DARK TIME

SUMMER COOPER

Copyright © Lovy Books Ltd, 2019

Summer Cooper has asserted her right under the Copyright, Designs and Patents Act 1988 to be identified as the author of this work.

This book is a work of fiction. Names and characters are the product of the author's imagination and any resemblance to actual persons, living or dead, is entirely coincidental.

In no way is it legal to reproduce, duplicate, or transmit any part of this document in either electronic means or in printed format. Recording of this publication is strictly prohibited and any storage of this document is not allowed unless with written permission from the publisher. All rights reserved.

Respective authors own all copyrights not held by the publisher.

Lovy Books Ltd
20-22 Wenlock Road
London N1 7GU

1

EMILY

"*E*mily, wait!" I heard him call out behind me just as the elevator reached the penthouse floor.

I turned my head, a small flutter of hope in my heart. I saw Dylan there, and the flutter in my heart became quiet as the beats thudded to a halt. His strong face, with features even Jensen Ackles would envy, was schooled into an uncertain expression. My fingers twitched. What was he going to say? Would he spew more angry words at me, or would he ask me to explain?

Please ask me to explain, I thought, but didn't say out loud. I looked at him and felt a knot form in my stomach. His dark hair was hanging down into his eyes, and I wanted to brush it away. My fingers twitched, my feet clenched in my sandals, but I held myself in place.

Dylan had just discovered my most hidden secret, and this moment would either make us or break us. He knew who I was. He now knew who my family was, but more importantly, who my brother was—an enemy he'd never asked for. Who could blame the man for that initial expression of betrayal that he'd worn on his face? Or the pain that turned his gray eyes into storm clouds. Those clouds had eventually blended into questions, questions that he wanted answers to.

I'd give him those answers, so long as he'd let me stay there with him. "Dylan?"

"Why, Steph ... Emily? Why the lie?" He scrubbed at his jaw with his palm, pain etched all over his face, a gut-wrenching replacement for the anger that had been there moments ago.

"I..." but I stopped. I looked around the foyer as I held the elevator door open, I didn't want to do this out here. I let the door close and waved around. "Not out here. Please."

It wasn't like anyone would see us, but this just felt too open to prying eyes for me. The things we needed to talk about were private matters, things that needed to be said where nobody else could hear. Where no witnesses could overlook your most broken moments. Because I knew that if he offered me a reconciliation, it would come at a cost. I sniffed as tears stung the back of my eyes and somewhere high up in my nose.

My prompt spurred him back into life. "Come back in. Let's talk about this."

"Alright." If it had been anyone else, the pure bile he'd spit at me when I walked into his living room only moments ago would have had me hauling ass out the door and into the elevator, but this was Dylan. My heart and soul. I'd stand there for the rest of my life if he wanted me to.

The sound the door made when it closed was loud in the quiet room, I was so afraid. Not afraid of him, I knew what Dylan was capable of, and harming me on purpose out of anger wasn't one of them. My fear came from my own worry that I'd make a mess of it all, that I'd get defensive and wouldn't use the same techniques I'd learned to use long ago with my father and brothers.

The same thing that let me walk into the living room with my head bowed in submission and led me to sit on the floor, by the arm of the couch. He always sat on the end closest to the wall, and that was where I arranged myself now.

"No, Emily. There, please." I looked to where his hand pointed and for a minute, my heart broke. He didn't want me at his feet. He wanted me further away, at the other end of the couch. Where I couldn't touch him?

I didn't protest; instead, I did as I was instructed and sat at the other end of the couch. I dropped my bag at the side of the couch and pulled my upper lip between my teeth to keep myself quiet. I folded my hands in my lap and crossed my ankles. The black Hermes sandals weighed my feet down, and the tight material of the dress made it hard to move around too much so fidgeting would not be a problem. I kept my head bowed and waited.

"Explain it to me, Emily." He sat at the other end of the couch and when I glanced to the side, I could see he was faced toward me. I took a deep breath and looked at the picture still frozen on the screen.

Ember and Kevin, smiling into the camera, happy and on top of the world. Behind them, I stood with a baby in my arms, my face tight and pinched. The baby had kept me up the night before with colic, while they'd slept the night away in a separate hotel room. Then we'd made a mad dash around the country, me still with the baby in tow because they wouldn't let me take their daughter back to their house in Nashville. They didn't want her too far out of their sight, and I couldn't blame them, but the traveling didn't help the baby's colic at all. I'd wanted to burst into tears the moment that picture had been taken because I'd felt like I had the weight of the world on my shoulders, and no way to get out of the situation I was in.

"I think that picture explains it all, Dylan." I limply pointed at myself with my right hand, then continued. "I was always in the shadows, behind my brothers. Never in the light."

"Okay. So you were the poor little rich girl. I get it. How did that lead you to me? What have you told Trent about me?" His jaw tightened, and I wanted to warn him he'd crack his teeth if he kept that up, but I didn't allow myself to do that.

I stared at him, anger in his dismissive tone made my eyes narrow. He had no idea about my life, but because he was angry, he got to judge me.

"No, I don't think you do get it, Dylan." I turned toward him, a little bit of backbone coming back into my posture. "I spent my entire life taking care of those jerks, and where did it get me? They didn't even remember my birthday this year. They knew my number when they needed me, when their kids needed looking after, or before, when they'd thrown a party that had gotten too out of hand and someone needed to calm the police down, but otherwise? I wasn't a member of the family. I was the nanny, the fixer, the one who took care of all their problems. I gave my entire life to them, yet, not a single one seemed to actually care about me."

I swiped at a tear I didn't want to shed. I didn't want to be pitied, I wanted to be understood. "I didn't know what actual love was until my nephews and nieces came along, and I fell in love with them. That's when I knew what love really was. As the years went on, and I didn't have time to go on a date, much less have a long enough relationship to make a baby of my own, I decided I wanted some of that for myself. I wanted a relationship, a man who made me feel alive, loved, and wanted. Maybe not permanently, but I wanted to experience it. Or the illusion of it, at least."

I paused, took a deep breath, and lifted my eyes to his. "I met Roxie at a charity event I went to, and we became friends. She told me about her world, about the club, and that made this itch start inside of me. I wanted to be free. I wanted to be the kind of *alive* she told me about. The kind where you didn't travel across America at the whim of your family or go to bed with snotty kisses on your face and puke all over you because you're just too tired to take a shower or change clothes. I wanted the world she whispered to me about with fire in her eyes."

"It was Roxie who set this up then?" His eyes narrowed, and I could see the wheels turn in his mind. I wanted to nip that assumption in the bud right away.

"No. She set it up so that I could go to the club, yes, but the rest? I wanted to find myself a happily ever after when I first started to think about moving on from my family, but then I thought—why go straight into the same kind of life I wanted to leave behind? Why not have some fun, be bad, and see what life has to offer first? Why not be a little wild before I make myself someone's nanny all over again? Roxie didn't have anything to do with that. She didn't plot with my brother to get us together either. The two have never met." The firm tone and the look I shot him made no bones about that.

He nodded, and I could see a slight bit of color creep up his neck as I stared him down. Good, he should feel a bit of discomfort for even thinking any of this. I couldn't blame him, not really, but that didn't make it right.

"So, Trent didn't..." He stopped, and he had the good grace to wince at his own logic.

I sighed heavily and clenched my fingers together tighter. I wanted to whack him on the arm with something, but thought if I touched him the whole truce we'd called might shatter.

"Do you really think Trent Thompson would send his little sister into an adult club to make a whore out of herself just to humiliate you, Dylan?"

"You aren't a whore," Dylan said immediately as he leaned toward me.

That gave the hope in my heart a reason to grow, but I kept it in check.

" That's what you're implying, Dylan. That my brother sent me to you to whore myself out in order to spy on you." Now that I'd said it out loud, it really hurt. This time the tear that streaked down my face burned hot, and I swiped at it angrily.

"I guess that is how it sounds." He sighed and leaned against the plush back of the couch, his right thumb and forefinger in his eyes. "Fuck, where did this all go wrong?"

"You assumed. A lot of people do that when it comes to me." Now that his fury had passed, my own started to build. It wasn't really logical, but now that I'd said it out loud, it made me angry that he'd thought I'd let someone do that to me. Or that my brother would sink that low.

Well, to be fair, Trent had been a huge dick lately, so maybe it wasn't so far-fetched, but still, to think that I'd do that?

"I'm sorry. It was just ... a shock." He pulled his hand away and looked at me. His eyes were red from his rubbing, but they were the same gray eyes I'd come to adore so much.

My anger fled, hurt the final negative emotion to remain. I wasn't sure how long that would take to ease, but I knew I wasn't out of the woods yet.

"I know. By the time I figured out who you were, by the time Trent had even mentioned your name in my presence, it was too late. I didn't know you, not really, and all he said was some complaint about you being here. In his town. Whatever that means." I left off the part about patricide and kept quiet for a moment.

"I guess I mentioned Trent a time or two myself. So it's not totally out of the realm of possibility for Trent to mention me. Yes, after our first meeting, I guess it was kind of hard to tell me who you really were. Not just because of your family, but because I could have used that as leverage against you."

"I don't think you'd ever do that, Dylan." I started to reach out to him but pulled my hand back. "It's just not who you are."

"No, you're right." He got up, his eyes still on the screen, and for the first time I saw realization dawn on his face as he looked at me, hidden in the shadows. "You know, I saw the same thing on your social networks, and it didn't really hit me until now. The only time you aren't in the shadows is when you have a kid in your arms. The rest of the time ... wow. That is pretty shitty of your family."

He turned and looked down at me, sadness in his eyes.

"It's nothing like your story." I interrupted whatever else he'd meant to say.

"Well, no, it's not. We all have our burdens to bear, in our own ways." He didn't even question how I knew exactly what his story was.

I'd learned it from the things he'd said and from the news stories I'd found online. He'd had a traumatic childhood, and mine would never compare with his, but as he'd said, trauma was relative.

"It's hardly surprising you wanted someone to see you, Emily."

The way he said my name, as if it was unfamiliar but already adored, made me smile. "I just wanted to feel alive, more than anything, Dylan.

You do that. You made me feel real, and I didn't want to lose that over who my family was. I wanted to tell you, I planned to tell you tonight, but you beat me to it. Or, Ember's new album beat me to it."

He shoved his hands down in his pockets and breathed in deep and slow. "What do we do now?"

"Well, I've officially been kicked out of my family. You remember that day when we saw Trent? That was the day he figured out I was seeing you and convinced my father to disown me."

"Wait, what? He fucking did what?" Dylan stood. His anger made his gray eyes darker somehow, and I could feel the waves of his emotions as he stood over me.

"He convinced my father to…" I had to pause. My throat closed up tight, and white-hot tears leaked out of my eyes like traitorous little diamonds. I put my hand over my mouth as reality set in, and pain tore through me. I'd never see any of them again.

"Emily, Jesus, why didn't you say anything to me, woman?" He came to me, knelt in front of me as I bent over my knees. Pain made my stomach ache, and my head swam as I tried not to sob. "Baby, please. Don't make yourself sick."

That's when I started to sob.

2

DYLAN

She betrayed you. She lied. She didn't tell you the whole truth. Words and emotions swirled within me as Emily curled in on herself, her emotions out of control. She'd broken, and I hadn't exactly meant to do that. Sure, part of me felt justified, felt as if she deserved to be so remorseful. She cried her eyes out, but it gave me no real satisfaction to see it come to life.

The man I was two months ago wouldn't have cared. He might have even felt some satisfaction in watching a woman break down into tears, but that wasn't the same man I was now. This moment brought me no joy, and I couldn't let her carry on, so completely lost.

As I watched the only lover I'd ever cared about fall to pieces before me, I forgot the betrayal and anger I'd felt and tried to ease her discomfort. I wrapped my hands around her shoulders and pulled her into my arms. She didn't resist at all; rather, she fell into my arms, and her face found its home in my neck.

"Shh, Emily, calm down, please. You will make yourself sick."

I tried not to think about the way I'd felt, or how much I wanted to kill her family for making her cry like this. At that point, the fact that she'd hidden who she was from me, kind of made sense. She'd wanted a moment of not being a Thompson, of not being the sister/caretaker/nanny. She'd just wanted to have what even her brothers had been able to have. A fucking life.

I held her to me and let her cry herself out. We'd talk about the rest of it later. For now, she needed to know she was in a safe place, more than I needed to rampage like a wild animal because she'd kept her identity a secret from me.

I even liked her real name more than the one she'd given me. Emily suited her perfectly. I sat on the couch and pulled her into my lap. Her body was swathed in mine, and for this moment the world couldn't harm her. I kissed the top of her head as the sobs finally began to taper off.

I'd had a shitty upbringing, there was no doubt about that. My mother was, at the very least, psychotic. My father had wanted to keep her calm and happy, but he'd only made matters worse. The end of their lives had almost brought me peace. It brought me the couple that gave me a new chance at life and gave me all the love they could. The tragedy that was my early childhood had become a triumph.

Emily's misery had gone on her entire life, and for whatever ridiculous reason, none of her family did anything about it. From the way she described, and the photo evidence I'd seen, she was their whipping boy. It infuriated me that the moment she stood up for herself and demanded some respect, they'd shut her down. She didn't have to explain it any more than she had. It wasn't just me who had angered Trent, it was the fact that she'd tried to have a life of her own for once that had really pissed him off.

"What is wrong with your family?" I asked softly, half hoping she wouldn't hear me because I didn't really want to set her off into a flood of tears all over again. The question felt almost cruel, and I winced when she slid off my lap, running her fingers through her hair.

"Oh, they've been fucked up since day one. My father's first wife, Trent's mother, died when she was young, and my father replaced her with my mother. I think my mom was meant to be a trophy wife, someone to fill his empty arm when he went to social functions. Sure, he had a few more children with her, but I would never say my parents were in love, or even liked each other. Respect, yes, definitely, but anything else? No. They lead such different lives."

Her face was red and splotchy, but I didn't care, she was still beautiful, even if her makeup was smudged and her face was wet. I ran into the bathroom, wet a facecloth and brought it to her. She took it as I settled on the couch beside her.

"Your mom didn't show you love then?" I knew rich women could be cold, but to their own kids? Well, yes, I thought after a moment, I'd seen it at boarding school.

"No, she was always too busy with my father; love was the nanny's job. The nanny was busy with my older brothers, and Trent was a handful from the word go. He hated my mother, he hated us, and he hated his dad for making more babies. My entire life I've tried to keep the peace between them all. I had to grow up early and play my part. Maybe it's my own fault." She let her head fall back and swiped at her face with the cold, damp cloth.

"So you were always in control, never able to let down your guard, and always ready to take command if you needed to?" I could see it now, why she wanted the relationship we'd had. She'd had a confusing life of total control one moment and none at all the next.

With me, she'd had a defined relationship, based on the fact that I'd be the one always in command;

she wouldn't have to make any decisions at all. I could see how that would be appealing to her.

"It was like living on a merry go round or a seesaw, Dylan. I never knew where I'd wake up next, which child I'd have, or which brother I'd be chasing after. The wives tried to help, after they came along, but they're all so..." she paused to shiver with something I took to be disgust, "...in love."

When she'd finished, and the crystal-clear gray of her eyes was on me again, I could see the shiver hadn't been disgust but sadness. She'd been abandoned all over again, this time by the women who should have worked really hard to make her feel like part of the family, not just another servant. Instead, they'd fallen into the same pattern of trying to play catch up with the brothers. Emily had only been a face, not a real person, to them.

She took a deep breath, and I could see the way she gathered herself. This must be what she did when life became overwhelming with her family. She'd have a moment to cry and then get on with life. Not a bad way to deal with it, but she shouldn't have had to do it so often. She smoothed her hair, swiped at her face, and took a deep breath. She gave me a weak smile, and her hands fluttered for a moment as she tried to think of what to say next. I could almost see the moment she decided what she wanted to say. Her eyes became clear once she'd chosen a path, and she looked much calmer.

"Anyway, if you don't want to kill me now, I brought this over." She reached around the edge of the couch and pulled her bag into her lap.

She dug around inside the contents of the huge, black leather bag and then brought out the folder I'd left the contract in this morning. I could feel a racing thump in my chest and put my hand over the spot. My hands shook a little as I reached for the folder, and that made me snatch the file from her.

I hadn't meant to snatch the file away so quickly, but I didn't want her to see my hands shake like that. I dropped the folder and cast a glance up at her face to see if she'd noticed. That mixed with the way my heart raced made me wonder if something was wrong within me. *A symptom of my condition, again?* I brushed it aside as nothing but nerves from the last hour of emotional upheaval and opened the file.

She'd signed it at some point in the day, and I looked down at the words I'd written there. She had virtually been a prisoner her whole life. Was it fair of me to ask her to sign anything like this now? I could understand now why she'd hated the idea of a contract so much. I brushed my hands through my hair and started to speak.

"Emily?" That was when it occurred to me, she'd signed the contract with her real name.

I looked at her and saw the truth there. She really had planned to tell me about this. Still, the betrayal was there. The emotion wasn't as intense now, my brain no longer felt as if it was melting, and my heart wasn't as crushed, but she'd kept a very important secret from me. What was to stop her from doing that again later, if she felt it was important?

You can't trust other people. The words danced around in my mind, a memory from my youth, in those dark days after my parents died. The days when I'd withdrawn into myself. I'd done it to try to protect myself from the knowledge that my mother had tried to kill me; that she'd succeeded in killing my father and herself. Trust meant weakness, weakness meant death.

Trust no one, that had been my motto from that point on. I'd allowed a few people into my life since those dark days, but not many. Now, I was stuck, addicted to a woman that I couldn't get out of my system. Like a heroin addict who couldn't stop shooting up, even when their veins had collapsed and their limbs had turned gangrenous, I still couldn't give her up. Every instinct in me, all the knowledge I'd gained over the years, the protective measures I'd put in place to wall off my heart, said to let her go, that she was trouble; she was a

Thompson, get rid of her. My heart, and to an extent, my brain, said the opposite, though.

"Emily, this is..." I couldn't continue. I couldn't admit that she could break me, that she might break me, because that would be weak. The truth of it was there, though, even if I turned away to hide the evidence that had to be on my face.

I hadn't cried since I was a child, and I wouldn't now, but there was something stinging my eyes. I blinked until it passed and hardened my jaw. Suddenly, I knew what I had to do. Even though she'd hidden her real identity for very good reasons, I couldn't let her see me as weak. It was my job to take her control, to give her direction, and to make her life less complicated.

"Get on your knees, Emily." I stood and walked away, and she did as I instructed.

I left her there, pretty as could be, and went into the kitchen to get a drink to cool my throat. She could sit there, with her thighs trembling and her knees aching, until I was ready. Until I could control myself.

The way I felt right now, calmly out of control, was too contradictory. I might hurt her if I took her into that private room of mine at this moment. I'd make her wait, make her wonder. There was no doubt now, she was mine for as long as I wanted her, but I'd let her sweat it out.

A smile played at my lips as I went in to fetch

the necklaces I'd bought her. I took them into my bedroom and left them on the dresser I'd had brought in for her use. She could take them later. I made sure everything was ready, and then I went into the hallway.

"Emily, take off your shoes and dress. Leave them beside you," I called out to her from the doorway. Her eyes shot to mine, and I saw anticipation written on her face. I didn't think she would ever ask me to take her to my private room, and I wasn't sure she craved it the way I wanted her to, but she would never tell me no. Mainly, because she needed to have that domination as much as I needed to dominate.

In the lingerie she'd chosen, dominating her would be more than a pleasure. Tiny black scraps of cloth covered her most intimate areas, and I had to admire her choices for the night ahead. The material enhanced the loveliness of her skin and became wrapping that I would soon enjoy tearing into. Although, it did look like something I'd want to have her in again, so maybe not so much tearing.

For a moment, as I took in how lovely she looked in her black bra and panties, I saw defiance tighten her jaw. Her eyes flicked to the contract, now on the floor, and then back to me. We'd both signed it now, and she'd agreed to my terms. Acceptance settled onto her features, and she moved. The shoes were kicked off, and the dress was pulled over her head. She folded the dress and set it on top of her shoes, beside her, as I'd instructed.

Her chin came up as she moved into position, and I smiled a pleased smile. Her face was blank now, ready for me to fill it with my creations. Lust, pleasure, pain would all take the place of defiance and acceptance. When I chose to give those things to her. "Stay there."

I walked out and went into the kitchen. I'd stopped cooking for her when the news came on the small television in the kitchen. I'd turned everything off, so now I'd finish it up. We'd have dinner, and we'd finish this night off. My hands shook again, a slight tremor, as I picked up the knife to move vegetables into the now heated pan.

That stupid illness again! I'd have to talk to my doctor, have him flown out here or something. This couldn't carry on.

I let my worries go and focused on cooking. Playtime had already begun, but I wanted to feed her before I really got the show on the road. She'd need her strength.

EMILY

An hour later and I was on my knees again. I'd been fed a very lovely dinner, and Dylan had even brought out a nice bottle of red wine to go with it. We'd had a quiet and uneventful dinner. The quiet from his side of the table almost drove me mad, but I knew I had to be patient.

I'd seen Dylan in odd moods before. He'd usually take me to his private little room and find rather creative ways to make me scream his name. I knew that was where we were headed tonight. I didn't protest, and I didn't ask for forgiveness. He would give me that when he was ready and in his own way. Besides, when the end result of his playroom antics meant I'd have a night of mind-blowing pleasure, why would I protest?

This was his way of coming to terms with his

problems, a rather creative way, but still a coping mechanism. If it brought both partners some enjoyment, what was the problem with it? I wiped at my mouth delicately after I brushed my teeth and reapplied my lipstick. The line was perfect, and the color, a deep burgundy that was too dark for me to wear out in public, was one Dylan had chosen. He loved to smear it across my lips in the playroom, and I liked to accommodate him.

It wasn't exactly how I'd pictured the night going, and from the rose petals I'd seen strewn over the bed, I knew it wasn't what he'd had planned either, but fate had decided that tonight would either make or break us. So far, it hadn't broken us. I didn't think.

I let my hair down around my shoulders and opened the bathroom door. He stood there, waiting for me, his head down and his hands in the pockets of a pair of dark gray flannel pajama bottoms. He had on a black tank top that stretched across his muscular chest, and I had to clench my nails into my palms to stop my hands from reaching out to touch his exposed skin. His head came up, and his dark hair fell back away from his eyes.

I loved his eyes, rimmed with long, thick black eye lashes. They bored into mine like a laser, and I inhaled sharply. I'd seen a look like love there for a second, but then it was gone.

"Are you ready?" he asked, his voice low and

quiet. There was no need for nervousness or to shout. It was only us, and nobody could hear us.

"I'm ready, sir." I smiled a dark, enigmatic smile. Almost the smile of an automaton, but not quite. I bowed my head and took his hand as he led me to the playroom.

The fact that the flower petals did not lead to this room told me that he hadn't planned the night to take us here, but that was where we were. There was no going back now.

My eyes darted around the room, to the cuffs embedded in the walls, the barrel he'd sometimes tie me to. The special table that was shaped like an "x" that would allow the dom to spread the arms and legs of the sub or close them tightly with the push of a button. Then there were the implements of pleasurable torture that he had available. Whips, straps, floggers, clamps, and even a variety of plugs for various orifices were all displayed along one wall and on numerous black shelves. This room could bring you pain, pleasure, or a mixture of both.

Dylan let me stare at the room, left me to wander as he inspected his implements. I stood still and waited for direction. I didn't question him or ask where he wanted me to go, because I knew he would tell me when he'd decided. He would lead me, as was his duty.

"Here," he said after a long wait. My brain had

gone quiet, inactive, as I waited, but now it went on alert, and I jumped to answer his demand.

I went to the barrel and waited for his touch. He would guide me in every move I made from here until we walked out of this room.

"I will buy you a new pair of these, because I have a feeling I will destroy them tonight." His fingers came down, a warm caress, as he slid a finger lower on my abdomen, between my skin and the edge of my panties. I held a breath and waited; would he tease me now? Would he touch me there, to prime me for what was to come?

I felt relief as my bra was unsnapped, and cool air washed over my breasts. He'd removed my bra, at least. He gripped at my breasts for a moment before he removed them and gently pushed me down with a touch between my shoulder blades. "Face down, Emily."

I guided my hands to the cuffs along the broad wooden barrel, and he clamped the closures shut. My head was down now, and my feet had left the floor. Each of my ankles was closed in the same kind of fleece-lined cuff, and my capture was complete.

I heard Dylan move and then saw his knees as his body came into view at my head. The barrel was really quite large, even if it was only half of the thing. The wood had been sanded smooth and varnished so that I wouldn't get splinters, but it was still a rough texture against my delicate skin.

"For now, I want your senses attuned to only what you feel, Emily. It's still odd to call you that, you know. It does seem right, somehow. Emily. I like it. Let's make you mine all over again now." He placed a blindfold over my eyes, little more than a scrap of leather that blurred out the light and my view.

He went further than that. He put a ball in my mouth, and I felt the ties go around my head. I almost protested, the ball always made my jaw sore later, but I held it back. When I felt him push something into my ear, I almost jumped, but I held myself quiet, submissive with a desperate clutch at control. My hearing became muted.

Until he put the other earplug in.

Now, I couldn't hear much of anything at all. I did feel his fingers as they skated down my back, along the curve of my buttock, and down to my thigh. He must have followed the path of his hand because next, I felt the breath of hot air as his lips came down on my skin. Just where my ass and my thigh met.

My back curled, eager to accept his touch. I knew where this was going, and I wanted him to begin. I needed him to begin.

I'd come to him as a new woman tonight. I was

Emily now, not Stephanie, the waif he'd picked up at an exclusive strip club. I was Emily, a woman who didn't need his money or his name. I only needed what he could give me. Controlled pleasure, domination of my every thought and feeling, and the ability to submit who I was to someone else for my own gain.

Dylan was my master, totally now, because I'd given him that power. My toes curled when his lips brushed along my ass. Would he make me come so soon? Or was this just a moment in the long tease? I wanted to move. My hip ached a bit, pressed into the wood, but I endured it. Any movement now could be seen as rebellion, if it wasn't in response to a touch.

Dylan moved, and I felt alone. In the darkness, I waited, my brain turned off again, but my body wasn't. Far from it, in fact. I could feel the juices of my excitement already soaking into my panties, and a heat burned from my nipples and down to somewhere in my lower abdomen. The heat made my nipples tight and achy as they pressed into the hard plane of the wood. My head rested against the barrel, my right cheek pressed into the wood.

I could see a glare of light along the top edge of the leather over my eyes, but nothing else. I wanted to feel something already, anything, and impatience began to course through me. I controlled it. I controlled my urge to moan out an order to him or a request that he touch me. I clamped down on it the same way I clamped my jaws down on that ball.

I inhaled and made my toes uncurl. That was when I felt the first slap of something flat and thin. It was a sharp sting against my ass, and I couldn't help the loud gasp that escaped my throat then. It stung, it itched, it made me so damn wet!

Then another lash across the other globe of my bottom, and I knew it was the hardened piece of leather, about an inch and half wide, but almost a foot long. It was designed to leave marks, to make the sub itch and burn with desire at the same time.

I felt Dylan's nails rake across my skin, and I knew he was inspecting the welts he'd created. I knew the skin would be pink and angry, a color that tempted him. Again, the explosion of pain, so close to my pussy, and the world tilted. He'd moved the barrel so that my ass would be higher in the air, while my head would be much lower. My feet were flat against the barrel, and the cuffs on my ankles held me in place and kept me from sliding off the surface.

He struck me again and again, almost a frenzy of blows, and my ass began to burn. Yet, the pain and the itch made my pussy throb and ache for more. I wanted him to hit me there, to make the blows land over my lower lips, to touch against my clit. I wanted to squirm, to draw his attention to my needs, but I knew that would just make him stop.

I needed so much, but I couldn't ask for it. Not yet. I still had panties on, but I felt them go now. A slide of metal, a snip, and the delightful black panties fell around one ankle. I'd really liked them, but I could get another pair. For now, my skin was totally bare, and I knew that meant there was more to come.

A new sensation grabbed my attention as I felt something thick slide into me, an inch at first, and then deeper. It wasn't Dylan's cock, I knew that from the coolness of the object, so it must have been one of the dildos he had bought to use on me. I shook a little, but that was from pleasure, not fear.

Dylan wasn't the kind of man who was afraid to experiment, obviously, and his goal through his domination of me was to take away my ego, to make me a canvas for his art. His art was giving me pleasure.

I shuddered when the dildo went in deeper, and his hand came up against my skin. I felt the heat of his skin against my inner thighs, and I moaned as he pushed into me all the way. I wanted him to move it within me, to fuck me with this thick, hard object. It felt good, but I knew what would make it better. His cock in my ass.

That wasn't what he gave me, however. His

hand held the dildo in place, while his other hand came down flat on my ass. I moaned around the ball in my mouth and felt my eyes roll back in my head. He was going to make me work for it then.

I lost control of myself and moved against my bonds. I pulled at the cuffs and tried to talk around the ball but couldn't. Another slap jolted me back to my senses, and I knew my protests would only earn me more. Was that a bad thing?

I couldn't hear, I couldn't see, I couldn't speak; all I could do was feel and smell. I would catch the faint hint of Dylan's cologne, the smell of the wood and leather in the room, but little more. I couldn't smell his skin or touch it with my mouth to taste it. I could only hang there and wait for his art.

His hand came down on the small of my back, but not as a strike. Softly, he splayed his hand on my skin and soothed me. I stopped my protests, and the momentary bad behavior calmed. I guessed he decided to give me a reward because something changed. A buzz began in my nether regions, and I knew it had to be the dildo.

He'd turned something on, and a warmth began to join with the buzz. A muffled moan came out of my throat, and my hips tensed. His fingers, still on my back, stroked me to keep me calm. I felt some movement between my thighs, and my head came up when his lips touched me. I knew it was his lips because I felt the moist stroke of his tongue on my clit.

My fingers clenched in the cuffs, and I made some kind of sound, but it wasn't protest; it was pleasure that drove me to react. A good sub would stay still, remain quiet, but I couldn't be that good sub. I could only do what Dylan drove me to. I was still me, for now.

His tongue tickled at the throbbing organ, eased the ache, but made it worse at the same time. It combined with the buzzing warmth inside of me, and I almost lost my mind. I went to somewhere only Dylan could take me—a place of darkness, where I didn't exist, where there was only good.

Until he pulled away, removed the dildo, and slapped my pussy harshly. I'd almost been there, fully in the arms of heaven, but he'd pulled me away. Just one more lick, one more buzz would have sent me there directly, but he'd taken it all away.

I stayed completely still. I didn't move, didn't protest. Not even when he moved the barrel so that I could stand. He removed the cuffs and pulled me up. I inhaled deeply through my nose, and when I could stand properly, Dylan led me to the wall. He wasn't finished then.

My hands went up over my head, and I knew this would be the worst part of it, but ultimately the best. He was enamored with my breasts, and he loved the way I reacted to his touch. My nipples were super sensitive, and it excited him to know he could make me come with nothing more than a suck of each nipple.

I felt him pinch the right one before his lips closed over the bud. Heated wetness closed around it and became my world for a second. His tongue flicked at me, sucked at me, licked me, before he pulled away, and cold air puckered the already tight flesh. Something clamped down around it, something tight, that sucked at the aching flesh. Suckers, fuck, he'd put suckers on me.

Then he did the same to the other one, and I wanted to sink to my knees. I wanted to suck his dick. I wanted to fuck him. I wanted to ride him with wild abandon until I'd come so hard, I passed out. Thoughts, memories, fantasies flooded into my brain, and then, he placed one of the evil little fuckers on my clit.

Hot, white heat flooded into my brain, and my overstimulated nipples felt as if they might burst. It was too much, but it wasn't enough. Dylan knew that. He knew exactly what he could do to me, and he gave me everything I needed when he lifted me against the wall and fucked into me.

Hard, fast, with no real care about whether I came or not, Dylan was out of control by the time he fucked me. I screamed around the ball in my mouth, my hands still cuffed to the wall, but it was because I had started to come the second he thrust into me. His fingers dug into my ass as he held me up, but it was more pain, more pleasure, and I took everything he gave me, as I gave him everything I was. Every single part of me now belonged to Dylan. Even my name. Emily.

4

EMILY

A half hour later and I was in his arms, in a hot tub of water that eased the ache from my muscles. He held me to him, our damp bodies cradled together. I leaned my head back against him and sighed, happily.

I thought I'd lost him, that I'd lost that one bit of happiness I'd had in my life. I'd found that happiness for myself. I'd grabbed it and held onto it tightly, but I'd made a mistake. I hadn't told him the truth about who I was. That had almost cost me everything.

"No more secrets, Dylan. I promise you that." I spoke the first words I'd said since he'd asked me if I was ready to go to his playroom.

When he let me down from the wall, I'd been too drained to speak and had shaken my head positively when he'd asked if I was alright. I'd found the ability, and the strength, to speak again, and used it now to make a pledge to him. I'd never lie or mislead him ever again.

"You did it to protect yourself, and me, I suppose, Emily. You didn't do it to be malicious." I could feel his voice rumble in his chest and turned my head to listen to the sound better.

"I wasn't trying to manipulate you or spy on you. I just wanted to be with you." I sank a little lower in the water and let my ear rest against his chest. I turned around and looked up at him. "That's why I signed the contract."

"Have you actually read it?" He looked a little uncomfortable, but it had to be asked.

"I haven't, not completely." I looked away, uncertain. "I just wanted to sign it so you'd know that I was committed to this."

"The thing is, that wasn't just a contract for a lover, Emily. I want you here with me. To travel with me, to go out to places without a blindfold, and to explore the world with me."

"For however long you choose to keep me?" I couldn't keep the hurt out of my voice, but I did manage to maintain eye contact as I twisted to look at him better.

"That's just it, Emily." He sighed and looked away, before he reached down and pulled my face up to his. "I can't even think about spending a day without you. It hurts too much."

"I, well…" I didn't know what to say to that, so I kissed him.

Dylan James had just admitted that he didn't want to be without me. That was pretty momentous. The man who wasn't boyfriend material, who didn't want a relationship, he just wanted a fuck buddy before he moved on, had finally met a woman he didn't want to move along from.

Wow.

"Six months. It's a promise of six months," Dylan said, a light of laughter in those eyes. "It's a promise that I will do all that I can to make you want to keep me around for longer than six months."

"Oh, you think you can keep me interested, do you?" I asked in a voice that teased while my fingers danced up his chest to cup his cheek. "I'm pretty sure you can, but maybe you need to convince me?"

"I think the way you screamed around that ball gag earlier is all you need to remember, young lady. You came so hard I thought you might have bitten right through that thing." His eyes went a little darker, and his voice dropped to a huskier level as he spoke, and I had to admit, my body responded to his words.

There was no doubt in my mind I wanted to have a relationship with the man. I wanted all he would give me, and now that we had the problem of who I was out of the way, we could get on with it.

"It won't be easy, you know. I have a hard time with things like that." He took a deep breath and for a minute, I thought he'd get up and leave the tub. He managed to stay, though, but he changed the mood and insisted on washing my hair.

He scrubbed my hair and took delight in making it spiky and twisting it around with all the bubbles, but eventually he knew I was getting cold, and we used the removable shower head to rinse my hair. We both cleaned up and wrapped ourselves in the bath sheets he had in place of towels.

They were a luxury I'd used before, but knowing he'd bought them with me in mind made it special. They were a light pink color and so thick and long we could have used them for blankets. I had a smaller towel wrapped around my hair, and we went into the bedroom. Dylan turned on the television, and we found a movie to watch.

He was asleep before it finished, so I turned the movie off and went into the kitchen to find something to nibble on. I reheated some of the paella and read over the contract as I ate the dish with some French bread. He was right, the document was a promise, more than a contract.

He'd kept most of our rules in place, and there were provisions for if we wanted to change the dynamics of our play or our relationship, but for the most part, this was Dylan's solemn promise to see where this was headed. In six months, we'd go over it all again and decide if we wanted to continue.

There was no real mention of love, or devotion, but it was there. The simple fact that he wanted a relationship out of this, and not just a contract for sex, meant that he had far more in his heart for me than lust.

He just didn't know how to admit it. I couldn't blame him. The first woman that told him she loved him, tried to kill him. The woman who gave him life had killed his father in the process of trying to kill them all. That thought kind of soured my stomach, so I went into the living room. I stared out at the city in the distance.

She must have had some subconscious hope that Dylan would survive. That was why she'd told him she loved him, before she'd left. She'd outright murdered his father, but she'd only planned to burn her son to death. Had she hoped he'd escape the flames, and that was why she hadn't shot him as she did his father? I chewed at my lip as I thought about it.

What kind of madness had driven her to such an act? Not that any of it would ever make sense, but I had to wonder about it. I could imagine my mother agreeing to let one of her children be shunned, she'd done it, but would she ever try to kill me to prove her love for a man?

I couldn't imagine any of my sisters-in-law doing the same thing to their children. They all seemed like the kind of bear mommas who wouldn't let anyone hurt their children, for anything, no matter how old they would grow to be.

It hurt me to think of a much smaller Dylan, with innocence still on his face, lying there as his mother poured gasoline on the floor. He'd smelled the strong odor of the fluid and had fled out of his bedroom window.

Tears stung my eyes, and I had to put a hand over my mouth to hold back a sob for that tiny little face. How he must have looked standing there watching as his house burn. I didn't know if that had actually happened, but my brain conjured the image up, and my heart broke for that small little child.

Had he cried, screamed for his parents, or had he stood there coldly, without an emotion, in shock perhaps? I doubled over from the pain it caused me, and I felt Dylan come up behind me.

"Emily. What's wrong, darling?" He pulled me into his arms and sank down to the floor with me.

"How could you stand it, Dylan? My God, you poor man." I clung to him, babbling like an idiot, but he patiently soothed me and let me cry in his arms.

"I endured it the same way you're enduring your own family's rejection, Emily. I held my head up and carried on. It was all I could do." His voice was strained, but he didn't cry. I suspected he hadn't cried tears in a long time. He must have cried himself out centuries ago.

Then there was my own pain, my own rejection. We had something in common then, kind of. My family had shunned me. It hurt, it really hurt, but I had him, and that made it bearable. Almost.

Dylan curled around me and shushed me, kissed me, and then he picked me up to carry me to bed. He pulled me into his front, both of us on our sides, before he pulled the duvet over us.

"Emily, you're a strong woman. I've learned that about you. It's one of the things that draws me to you. Even when you submit yourself, you still have a strength that cannot be broken. At least, not by me. Maybe because I don't want to break it, I don't know, but you are strong, darling. Somehow, we'll make this right. I promise you that."

I wasn't quite sure how he thought we'd make my family accept my choices, or take me back into the fold, and to be perfectly frank, right now, I wasn't sure I was ready to forgive the callous coldness of the way they'd disowned me. I had tried to shield myself from the emotions that swirled like a hurricane around those thoughts. I'd been focused on Dylan, and that had made it all worth it.

Now that we were settled into some kind of truce, I had time to think about it all. It wasn't an easy thing to swallow, that my choice had led to their decisions, but if it meant I was with Dylan, then I could deal with it.

That didn't make the heartache of it go away. I'd probably have days where it still weighed on me, but I knew I could cope with him by my side.

I turned and touched his face, two pairs of gray eyes stared at each other in the near darkness. I could see the shine of his eyes, though, and knew he was looking at me.

"You are all I have now, Dylan." It was an admission I'd never really wanted to make, but it was true. We'd promised not to hide anything anymore, so I thought that meant our emotions were included in that promise. "You are really my world now."

"Then I'd better make it worth the price you paid, hadn't I?" His voice was level but held a certain amount of conviction.

"I wasn't trying to make you feel beholden to me, or like you owed me something. You don't. I just want you to know that you are all I have." I turned away, a little embarrassed now. "Fuck, that sounds clingy and so damn sad."

"No, it just sounds like raw emotion, Emily." He

pulled me back to face him. "You aren't a robot, Emily, and I don't want you to run around with some kind of cold, little heart that I can't crawl my way into. I want you to be real with me. To tell me how you feel, what you think, what makes you happy, what makes you sad. I want to know it all, Emily. I want to know you. If you hide these parts of you, I'll only know what you want me to see."

I still felt like I was on a pity party, but he kissed me and made it all better. His kiss was gentle at first, and I relished the sensation of his soft lips against mine. His kisses always felt so good.

I kissed him back, and soon the gentleness became insistent, and his lips opened above mine. Passion flared in an instant, and the need to have him drive me to that place only he could take me to took over. My arms wrapped around his shoulders, and he pulled me over him. I settled onto him and pressed my sex down into his hard length. He was ready for me in an instant.

There was nothing that could stop this passion, nothing that could keep us apart. There was always that one final part of our lives that could separate us, but right now, I had a feeling that death would be the only thing that could ever make this all end. I would fight even that to keep this.

5

DYLAN

One Month Later

The sound of the plane's engines nearly deafened me as the wheels met the tarmac, and we were suddenly on the ground again. I breathed a deep sigh of relief once the bounces had stopped, and the plane pulled into a terminal. It had been thirty days since I last saw Emily, and it was thirty days too long.

I stepped off the plane and headed straight for the car already waiting for me. A short drive to the penthouse and I'd have her in my arms. A call came in, and I punched a button on the console full of tabs and buttons, so many I hadn't figured them all out yet.

"Hello? That you, Mom?" I asked, I'd seen the number and knew it was likely my adoptive mother.

"No, it's your father. Did you make it back to that woman of yours yet?" My dad's voice, jovial if a little frailer than it used to be, filled the car, and I laughed.

"I have only just landed, Dad, trying to merge into traffic so I can get back to her right now."

"That's good then, son. We only wanted to make sure you made it back. Sorry we kept you so long."

"Oh, it's no trouble, Dad. You needed me." Dad had come from his trip to the hospital after a bout of pneumonia and was driving my mother crazy. I'd gone out to give her a hand until he got better.

To see my own doctor. He'd run some tests, and tweaked my medicine, and he was certain he'd have me back on track in no time now. I'd managed to kill two birds with one stone. Three if you counted my trips to our hotels on the west coast while I was out there.

"I'm glad you're keeping up with the business. I wasn't sure you'd want to take over for me, but you're doing a fine job, Dylan." I could hear the pride in his voice, and that made me smile.

I merged into traffic at last and headed in the direction of home. "I had a good teacher, Dad. Listen, I'll give you a call tomorrow, alright? I'm in a hurry to get home to Emily and to see how she is. I haven't told her I'm back yet, so it'll be a surprise."

"Oh now, son. That's not always a good idea, you know. Women, they like to dress up for a man, and if you catch her at home with her hair up in pigtails and no makeup on, well, she might be a little upset that you didn't give her the chance." Dad laughed, and I had to join him. That was a good piece of advice.

"You always were a smart man, Dad. I don't care what she looks like when I get there, as long as she's there."

"Well, don't say I didn't warn you." Dad laughed again, only this time there was a slight wheeze at the end. He was getting better but slower than I'd like. I worried about him often, but he insisted he was fine.

He was the man who had saved me from the foster care system, a system that might have destroyed me after what had happened to me as a child. He and his wife had taken me, and they'd treated me as one of their own, though, they had none of their own. It had been a life-raft for me, and I paid it back every day by being the son they deserved. I hoped I did anyway.

Dad let me get off the phone, at last, and I felt more comfortable. Even hands free, I believed that phone calls of any kind took your mind off the road, and I hated to do it. I had a lot to get home to, a surprise in store for my lady love. Two actually.

I'd finally acquired the building I'd been trying to buy for so long now. It was mine, all mine. I was excited to get started, and I had plans, so many plans. This would be my first hotel that was solely mine, and I wanted to do it right.

I wanted to involve Emily in that, and I planned to tell her the news, but something still made me hesitate. I didn't for a second believe she was involved in any trick now, but she was still a Thompson. A disowned one, but still. One of them might contact her, and she might let something slip...

Which was very disloyal of me, but finding out who she was, who she was related to, had really burned me. I didn't doubt her, not really; it was her vicious troll of a brother who I didn't trust.

I let him slip from my mind as I pulled into the parking garage and got my bags out of the trunk. I was tired, but not too tired. I couldn't wait to see her face.

The elevator seemed to take forever to slide down to my level and then, on the way up, I nearly banged on the walls I was so impatient. That wouldn't help it to go any faster, so I held back. It had been the longest month of my life, but it was done now, and a new part of my life was about to begin.

By the time I slid my key into the door and went into the hallway, I was ready for whatever she had to throw at me. I just didn't know that something would be her.

"Dylan!" she screamed my name, and all I saw was a white blur and some sort of pink before she was in my arms, wrapped around me as she planted kisses all over me. I fell back against the door, a very happy man.

"Oh my God, I can't believe you're here! Am I dreaming? Oh, please tell me this isn't a dream." She managed to get a few words in between her kisses, and I hugged her tight. She felt too good to let go.

"I'm really home, baby. Want to let me in so we can sit down?" She slid down and pulled me into the living room.

I could see now that she had on an oversized white hoodie and a tiny pair of pink shorts. Her skin was pale, but I liked that about her.

"I'm glad you've settled in." It had been part of the contract.

"I basically lived here before, so it wasn't a big deal. I've kept my own place, just because ... well, I just need to know it's there."

She gave me a look that I took to mean 'I hope you understand', and I did. It was sensible. We made it into the living room, and she pushed me down on the couch.

"Now, do you want coffee, tea, or me, dear sir?" She gave me a wink and a grin that nearly made my pants spontaneously combust. I'd only just walked into the place, but already I could feel that constant, never-ending urge to have her beneath me take over my thoughts. It didn't take much to do that when she was around.

I pulled her on top of me and laughed when she bounced a little. I teased at her lips with mine, and my hands cupped around her ass, just to tease her a little. I touched her softly at first, but I changed the pressure as her taste filled my senses. The sensation of having her on top of me, in my hands, made me as hard as a rock, with a deep need to bury that rock. With a low hum, I shifted my fingers to the edge of her shorts so that I could get my hands inside of them. "I was going to give you a surprise, but it can wait for a little while. I've missed the fuck out of you, Emily."

I heard a hum of approval from her and pressed up into her. "I need you so much."

I broke the kiss and licked my way down her neck. She inhaled sharply as my fingers pressed into her damp heat, and she leaned her head to the side to give me her neck. It was a submissive pose, one that opened her neck to danger, but my teeth would only nip at her skin, not pierce it. With a practiced move, I found the spot she loved to have sucked the most and gave it a quick nip before I closed my lips over it.

She groaned then, and that made my cock twitch in my pants. This wasn't going to last long at this rate, but I didn't care. I couldn't get enough of her, and she had obviously missed me as much as I missed her. Her hands rested on my shoulders, but they flexed over and over, as if to urge me on.

"You're about to get all you can handle of me, Emily." I pushed her down onto the couch, and she fell without a word of protest.

I whisked the tiny shorts from her body and had my face planted between her thighs in no time. I needed to have that taste on my tongue. I'd dreamed about it, I'd fantasized about it in lonely showers, and I needed it on my tongue now. My own pleasure could wait. For now, having her scent on my tongue as she rode my face was enough.

"Every single inch. After I make you come." I breathed over her bare skin, and I felt her shiver around me.

With a gentle finger, I explored her before I opened her to my mouth. My tongue took the place of my finger, and her taste flooded my mouth. She tasted like the food of the gods, and I took a moment to enjoy the taste of her on my tongue. Like a fine wine, I let the flavor of my woman fill my head. Or I did until she protested by clamping her thighs around my head.

With a knowing chuckle, I slid a finger inside of her and looked up just in time to watch her reaction. She moved so sensually, from the way her back arched to the way her breasts pressed against the cotton of her top. Her head was tilted back, but I could see the way her tongue came out to wet dry lips and when her hands came up to cup her breasts. I'd taught her that, to be a woman, to take what she wanted, and to touch herself without shame. Her hands pushed the top out of her way, and I moaned in helpless pleasure as her fingers tweaked at her rigid nipples.

I wanted her, I had to have her, and soon I would. When she'd flooded my mouth with her juices and screamed my name, I'd give myself exactly what I wanted; those sweet clinging walls of her wrapped around my aching dick.

I licked at her clit exactly the way she liked, until her hips moved in time with my tongue. Her breathless pants became much quicker, and I knew she was close. Even with our nightly talks, the dirty chats, and the orgasms she'd brought herself to while I watched, we still needed this. To be able to touch each other.

When she made a surprised sound, a sound of wonder and relief, I let her flood my tongue and ride my face. I moaned against her slick flesh, ready to have her, fuck, so ready to have her.

She hadn't completely come down yet, but I

couldn't wait any longer. As soon as she'd sighed in a certain way, the way she always did, and I knew she was almost done, I grabbed her hips and pulled her into me.

I slammed into her, hard, without mercy, her hips clamped in my hands. I fucked into her hard and fast without taking my eyes off of hers. The love in her eyes broke something in me, something I didn't know was even there, until I saw that look.

"You are mine, Emily." I felt her delightful grip at me, pull at me, and I wanted to stay inside of her forever. I moved, a deep thrust that made us both gasp, but I couldn't stop the words that forced themselves out.

"I'm yours, baby. So fucking yours." I pulled her up so that she could push down onto my dick while I impaled her from below.

"I'm yours, Dylan." I saw the love in her eyes, only stronger. She gripped her walls around me and moved her hips in time with mine. "For eternity."

I held her to me tightly, our bodies damp from sweat, but we didn't care. We were too lost in each other as our bodies moved in time together. I drove up, and she ground down until she gasped that sound again, and I knew I didn't have to control myself anymore. She shuddered above me, her thighs a tight vice around my waist, but I didn't care. All I could do was fuck Emily. It was what I'd been born to do.

The way her pussy gripped at me, tried to swallow me, and the sounds she made, sent me straight over the edge. I knew this would be quick, but I hadn't realized it would be that quick. I filled her with every drop of come I had to give and held her sealed to me.

I wanted to say things, things I'd never said to a lover, but I held them back. Even if I felt those things, I'd never said them, and it still felt like dangerous territory to me. What if she left me, got tired of my demands, my odd nature, and left? I couldn't take those words back, they couldn't be unsaid, and if I said them, it would make me weak.

"I, Emily, I'm so glad to be home." I'd almost fucked up, but at the last minute I saved the moment.

"I'm glad you're home too. Now, are you going to take me out and show me off or keep me all to yourself tonight?" She brushed my hair out of my eyes, and I kissed her on the lips.

"Whatever you want, darling." That was how it would be. Whatever she wanted to do. I'd save the surprises for later. In fact, I'd tell her one later, the other could wait a few more hours.

"Go get ready, I'll take you out to eat."

I smiled as she jumped away and headed for the shower. It was good to be home.

6

DYLAN

I ended up taking Emily and Roxie out that night. We went to eat, then we went to a new adult club in town. It wasn't Elmo's, but it wasn't bad. It was more about dancing and hooking up with strangers than it was about underground sex and exotic dancers. That was cool, but it didn't hold our interests for long.

"I'm going to get a taxi home, guys. I know you two want to get back to the privacy of your own home." Roxie put down the second drink she'd ordered and looked at us in the darkness at the end of the bar.

"I'm sorry, Roxie, I don't mean to ignore you." Emily turned to her friend and hugged her.

"You aren't, honey, I'm just not feeling this place." She looked around, her blonde hair a sway of gold down her back. "Besides, I think the clientele is a little young for my taste."

I looked around and saw that a lot of the faces were very young, almost too young from the looks of a couple. Maybe she was right, maybe we should get out of this place, and that wasn't just my dick talking.

"Listen, Roxie, let me drop you off. No need to waste money on a taxi. I have a little surprise for Emily tonight, so if you don't hear from her for a couple of days, it's because she's busy." I gave Roxie a knowing wink, and we both laughed.

"I don't need to know what you mean by busy, I just don't." She slapped my shoulder lightly and gave me a wide smile. She really was an attractive woman, but she wasn't my Emily.

"You ready, Em?" I asked, and she gave me a wink of her own.

"Anytime, baby."

Oh, that did do nice things to my dick. My eyebrow went up, and I couldn't help but smirk.

"You dirty little tramp," I hissed in her ear, and when I pulled back, I saw the most nasty grin on her face I'd seen yet.

"Only for you."

Fuck, how long was that flight?

"So what's the surprise?" Roxie asked as I pulled into her apartment block.

"Ah, that's still a secret, but Emily will be gone for a couple days. Don't panic, alright?"

They both looked at me, and I knew that wasn't enough. Damn. I'd wanted it to be a total surprise. I should have gotten Roxie alone to tell her.

"I'm taking her on a little trip. One that doesn't require many clothes." I looked at Roxie and knew the words had worked.

"Yep, that's all I need to know. Love you, Ems. Have fun, goodnight, and thanks for the ride." Roxie couldn't get out of the car fast enough, and we all laughed over that.

"See you soon, Roxie. Love you!" Emily called out, and Roxie lifted her arm up in answer. "That wasn't very nice."

The smile on her face said it had amused her anyway. It had me too.

"A man's gotta do, what a man's gotta do," I drawled at her in my best cowboy, before I put the car in drive and headed to the airport.

"What am I going to do for clothes?" she asked, and I looked over at her.

"Well, it's a last-minute thing, so there will be toiletries, some sleeping clothes, and going out clothes that I've ordered to be delivered to that address. They should be there already."

"Oh?" she asked, her voice quiet. "I hope it's somewhere cold."

I went still; surely, she hadn't guessed? Then, she'd said it often enough the last week or so. It was cool at the beach, but not cold. She'd missed the snow. I'd rented a cabin in the mountains of Virginia. Snow was guaranteed. All the snow she could want.

"I'm not telling until we get there." I took her hand in mine, kissed it, and headed for the airport for the second time that day.

I'd chartered a private flight for this trip, and it was ready when we got there. I looked down at Emily and smiled.

"Ready?"

"I'm not sure. I don't know if my clothes are appropriate." I remembered what my dad had said earlier, and I knew he'd been right about that part anyway.

"You'll be fine." She had on a pair of black leather Prada boots, a pair of leather pants, and a handmade, very expensive-looking, heather gray sweater that came down to her knees. The cowl neck made it look soft and warm.

Her eyes narrowed at me, but then she grinned as we climbed aboard the plane. "You're lucky I trust you so much."

"I don't doubt that a bit."

The plane took off after a few checks were made, and we headed off into the dark. Emily fell asleep before long, her head in my lap, and I just watched her sleep. She'd given all of herself over to me. She didn't have a fear in the world when I was with her. That was obvious from the way she slept so peacefully now.

The plane soon began to descend, and I woke her up gently.

"You know, I sleep so well when I'm with you," she said it quietly, and I knew her throat was dry. I handed her a bottle of water and decided to tease her a bit.

"Hmm, does that mean I'm so uninteresting that I put you to sleep?" I joked with an easy smile.

"No, I mean you make me feel safe, calm even. When I'm around my family, I'm always tense, on edge, waiting for the next scream or shout, the next demand that I fly off to take care of one of their kids or to clean up a new mess. I always felt *hounded*, really. With you, I don't have to worry about any of that. I know what you want from me, and I give it gladly. With you, I can relax." Her arms came up around my neck, and she gave me a kiss just as the plane bounced down.

A car waited for us at the airport terminal, and before long we were on our way up a slushy mountain road.

"A cabin in the woods, Dylan?" She looked at me with pleased eyes, and I knew I'd made her happy.

"Indeed, madam. Not one of those fancy ones with hot tubs, miles of windows, and views that can be seen from space. Nope, this is a tiny old place a friend of mine owns. It's a real cabin, but a nice one."

It was a nice cabin. A very small cabin, with one window, a room for a small bathroom, and another room for the bedroom where a king-sized bed was covered with a handmade quilt. A fire had been lit in the box stove, and it filled the tiny cabin with warmth.

"We're roughing it?" she asked, but with pure delight.

"Indeed, we are. Our kitchen is our living room, and there are no telephones. Cell phone will work, but not always. There's wood on the back porch, which has the view by the way, and we'll have to eat whatever my friend Tom brought and left in the fridge."

"Sounds just fine to me." She was staring at the bed, an old cast iron frame that was probably older than both of us combined. "This place looks like heaven to me."

Something had told me it would. Emily was a rich girl, that was true, but she wasn't spoiled. She wasn't the kind to worry too much about breaking a nail or being dirty, and I liked that about her.

"Hm, am I going to have to get out of the hotel business and buy us a cabin in the woods?" I purred down her neck as I wrapped my arms around her waist.

"You might, Dylan." She turned in my arms and looked at me with a look that confused me. She looked so sad.

"You've barely known me a few months now, but you know me so much better than anyone else ever has."

Ah, that explained the sadness.

"I listen to you, babe, that's why." I ran a finger down her cheek, to her collarbone.

She shivered, and her face went dark as desire flared to life, and that hit me hard. My own instant response was a grunt of need. I'd wanted to settle us into the place before I got her naked, but the way her breasts felt pressed into me made something ache deep inside of me. Only Emily could take that ache away, even if it was only a momentary relief.

I let my lips come down to hers, and the ache became a pulse of need that surged in my veins.

"Emily…" I whispered her name when I broke away, but I wanted to feel her tongue against mine and went back for more.

I had her pressed against a rough-hewn wall of the cabin when we finally came up for air. I looked down into light gray eyes, lighter than my own, but flecked with black from her passion.

"You know I'll always try to be the man you

deserve, don't you, Emily?" My thoughts calmed the rush of need that had flooded through me, but it didn't quite kill it. I doubted there was much on earth that could.

Her finger teased at my shirt buttons, and one popped loose to reveal a silky patch of skin. Her touch there distracted me, but now her eyes were on mine, and I couldn't look away.

"I want to be so much for you, but, I'm just not very good at it. I'm…" My words broke off, and I tried to find the right words for what I wanted to say. "I'm a broken man, Emily, but I'm trying fucking hard to not be, for you."

"You can only be what you are, Dylan. I don't need a man with no ghosts in his past, or a man who thinks he's perfect. I need you. A man who lives in the real world and knows how to listen to those he cares about." She brought her face up to mine and kissed away my moment of weakness.

Desire flared even hotter between us then, not the kind that had driven us into a frenzy on the couch earlier, or even the kind that had driven us to the wall earlier, but the slow kind that burned hot before it became an inferno.

My hand slid down the plane of her stomach, bare beneath the sweater she had on. I felt how hot and damp she was the minute my fingers slid into her panties, and it made me groan against her neck. Only Emily could do this to me.

I'd spent far too long fighting this. I'd tried to convince myself she was just a toy, but she was far more than that to me. I wasn't quite ready to step further than I already had, but Emily, my Emily, meant the world to me, and I wanted her to know that.

"Dylan, if you're going to fuck me, I wish you would before I die from wanting you." She purred the words as I picked her up and carried her to the bed.

"Don't you worry, baby, I'm just about to save you from that wasteful death." I pulled her sweater away, flicked the bra off of her body, tore her boots and those leggings off, flung it all away, and pulled my own clothes off.

When I settled down over her, my body between her thighs, I went on the offensive to drive death away. I bent down to circle a nipple with my lips, the way she liked. Her eyes went from her firm breasts to my lips before they closed with pleasure, and her head fell back. I thought I'd just fucked death right off.

I moved down her chest, but my little kitten had other ideas. She pushed me over, onto my back, and knelt between my legs. She made the most beautiful picture there, her face just over my cock as her bare ass waved in the light from an oil lamp left lit at the side of the bed.

My eyes focused on the pale flesh that had

never seen the harmful rays of a tanning bed. I liked how pale she was, how it was different from all the other women who spent far too much time worrying about a tan. Every inch of her body was pale and bare, and even if it wasn't, I wouldn't care. Emily was perfect, bare or not, pale or not. I could see from the way she bit her lip that she wanted to touch me, wanted to take control of the moment, and I'd let her have it, for now.

She took my dick in her hand and swallowed it down her throat so fast all I could do was hang on. I knew she'd practiced on me quite a few times, but this was new. She must have watched some videos while I was gone, and I wasn't about to complain. Not when I felt myself slide down her throat into those sweet, hot depths. Fuck, it was almost as good as fucking her, and if she kept it up, this game would be over with quickly. I wanted to tell her to stop but my hips surged up to push my dick further down her throat. If she wanted it, she could have every inch of me she could take.

I could feel how hard her nipples were as they pressed into my hard, muscular thigh. I wanted to have those nipples in my mouth, I wanted her to sit on my face so I could suck her clit, but fuck, all I could do was fuck her throat right now. Fuck, it felt so good, and damn if I didn't want to come all over her pretty face.

My head fell back as her tongue worked over me, and when her hand came up to touch the muscles that rippled in my stomach, I nearly came undone.

I fucked up into her mouth now, and her hands clamped over my hips and hung on as my hands dug into her hair to hold her head still. She was in control, but she wasn't. I was the one fucking her face, not the other way around, and she moaned around my dick. She loved it as much as I did.

Her hands slid under me to squeeze my ass, something I'd only recently learned I liked. Her fingernails dug into my skin as I thrust, over and over, until I was so close. Oh, so fucking close, and the little bitch nearly killed me when she pulled away.

"Emily?" I croaked, nearly dead from what she'd done. I was so close, fuck, I was going to die. I was so going to die.

She didn't say anything, so I opened my eyes and looked at her.

"That's an evil thing to do, Emily."

"What?" She leaned back onto the quilt, her legs open, tempting me.

"You know what," I growled and rose up over her.

I roughly flipped her over onto her stomach, and without a word, I settled her onto her hands and knees and fucked straight into her dripping body.

She'd teased me beyond control, and I knew that had been her plan when she moaned deep and loud with pleasure. I stabbed my hard length into her and pulled her hips tight so she couldn't move.

"That was a nasty little trick to play, just to get fucked, pet."

"It worked, sir." I heard the smugness in her voice and decided I'd spank it out of her later. For now, I just needed to come and to come hard. Her tight pussy was hungry, and it pulled greedily at my flesh as I slid out of her, as if it didn't want to let me go. I'd immediately pound into her, and when I heard that gasp, that oh so pleasing gasp, I found her clit and ground my thumb into it. The gasp came again, only it broke off just as my thumb began to make tight circles. She was about to blow.

"Take me with you, Emily, don't you come without me."

There was little she could do, but I fucked her hard and fast, until I felt it, that first tingle that said I was about to blow my load right there in her wet walls.

I came apart, and her body sucked me in to take me on that ride with her. Fuck, I loved the places she took me. Who would ever want to give that up? I stopped thinking then and blew into a million tiny pieces.

I heard her cry my name, somewhere far away, but I couldn't answer. My voice was gone, and all I could do was hang on until the force of this orgasm let me go.

7

EMILY

I thought something had changed between us when Dylan came back from Kansas. He was gentle those first few days, and even loving. Two weeks passed, and he got busy with his new hotel, which I was proud of him for. He'd beaten my brother at his own game, and I admired him for that. He'd told me about the new hotel while we were at the cabin, his face full of excitement and joy for the future.

I wished we were still at the cabin. There'd been one small window and a couch had been placed under it. I'd sit there for ages just looking at the snow, and he'd join me. It was peaceful, loving, and one of the best memories he'd given me so far. We'd even gone out a couple of times, and walked around, tossed a few snowballs around at each other. It had been playful, almost like we were teenagers falling in love for the first time. Those days had been sweet, and I'd come home with a lot of hope.

Then, something changed.

He'd come home in dark moods, and he wouldn't speak to me at all. He'd just type on his computer or phone until dinner was ready. When he was finished with his work, he'd take me into his playroom.

Last night had been one of those nights. He'd come home from a day at the hotel and hadn't said much. He'd complimented the dinner I'd made him and thanked me for it, before he'd led me into the playroom. I hadn't protested. It wasn't a horrible thing, but at the end, I felt as if I'd been punished.

He'd used language he'd never used before and had called me his little toy. At one point that would have thrilled me, but after he'd adored me so sweetly in the mountains, it kind of hurt to be back to this.

I had to wonder if he had to punish me for the fact that he loved me? He might not have said it, but I was fairly certain Dylan did love me. I was different to other women he'd been with. He kept me around, and he couldn't let me go. Either he was obsessed with me, or he loved me. Dylan was not the obsessive kind of guy, but he was protective. That was love, not crazy.

I sighed heavily and got up from the couch.

He'd come home tonight quiet, reserved, and gone to his swimming pool. I was waiting on him to come in before I served dinner. The lasagna would start to dry out of if he didn't come and eat soon. Finally, he did come out of the swimming room and into the kitchen.

"What's wrong, Dylan?" I asked as I set a plate in front of him. He still looked distracted, and I knew where the night would go.

"Nothing. Just, work. Thank you for dinner, it's lovely." He ate, but I doubted he even knew what he'd put in his mouth.

I cleaned up the plates and put the leftovers away. When he didn't get up, just sat on his phone texting someone, I went into the living room to read. I'd pulled a blanket over me to ward off the chill in the air. I settled in and got comfortable. I didn't even realize I'd fallen asleep until Dylan woke me up.

"I need you, pet. Please, come with me." He held his hand out to me, and I followed along behind him.

I wasn't prepared. I'd been asleep, but I followed along behind him. He turned the lights off, but soon he'd lit a few candles, just enough to illuminate part of the room with a golden hue.

"There, Emily." He pointed to a mat on the floor, and I knelt obediently.

As he'd done the night before, and the last time I

was in this room, he blindfolded me, inserted a ball-gag, and then he plugged my ears. A few times last night, I'd thought I heard him speaking, but I couldn't hear him. He'd taken the earplugs out eventually, and I'd heard the things he said. While they were thrilling, I'd also kind of wished he'd put the plugs back in.

He attached handcuffs to my wrists, and he pushed me down so that I was prone on the black mat. I had no idea where this was going to lead, but part of me wanted it. That had been the original attraction. He would be my master, he would rule me, and I'd have no say. To an extent, of course. Now I felt as if he wanted to punish me for something I hadn't done, or maybe I had. I hadn't told him about Trent or my family.

I turned my head so my right ear was pressed against the mat and waited. Dylan didn't do anything for the longest time. I waited patiently, unsure of what was happening. Dylan needed to work something out in his mind, and this was his version of doing that. I'd let him have his way.

I felt massage oil string along my back, cold but silky. He never warmed it, because he liked the reaction he got when I felt the cold liquid against my skin. My skin went over in gooseflesh, and I tensed. He massaged the oil into every inch of my back, worked out more than a few kinks I had, before his hands went lower. He indicated to me that I needed to lift my hands, and I raised them up as far as I could. His hands massaged beneath that area, and then he pushed my hands down.

Thank fuck, that was starting to hurt.

His hands probed deeper down my body, and the oil slicked the way as his fingers plunged down to coat my vulva with the oil. He spread it around, down my thighs, and back up. More of the liquid spilled onto my ass, and I knew where he wanted to go tonight.

I sighed and relaxed, the only thing I could do in this position. His fingers dug into the skin of my ass, kneaded it, until his fingers found the entrance hidden between them. One finger, perfectly manicured, teased at the puckered hole.

My hips arched back into his finger, my body on fire for the promise of that touch. Desire was like breath when it came to Dylan, no matter what he did it turned me on, and he knew that every inch of me was his. He could fuck me wherever he wanted, and I wouldn't protest, because I'd be too busy enjoying it.

His finger pressed against me, until the silky oil helped the digit to slide into my ass. Fuck, I shivered so hard when he first plunged into me. It felt like an invasion, every single time, but it also felt so damn good. My hips bucked again, a demand for more. A plea to please fuck my ass.

Dylan's finger slid deeper, and he began to

move in and out of me. It went deeper, further, and then there were two. His other hand found the entrance further down, and the mind-fuck really started. I could hear myself, panting his name around the ball in my mouth, but I couldn't say it, not really.

I wanted to, but he'd cut off our communication. This was how he wanted to fuck me tonight, and all I could do was let him. I let my mind go and focused on what he was doing. If he wanted to make me come so hard, I nearly broke my jaws on the damn ball he'd put in my mouth, then so be it.

I let my thoughts go and focused on his fingers. They were in my ass and in my pussy; he had filled all of me, almost. What I hadn't planned on was something thick, warm, but not his cock sliding into my ass. It felt like a real penis, but I knew there was no way this man would ever let anyone else fuck me. No way.

Yet, it still felt warm and silky, real even. He was beside me, so I knew it wasn't him, and there wasn't some mysterious ass fucking bandit behind me, so it must have been a plug or a dildo. I knew it was a plug when my puckered entrance closed around a much smaller end. He'd buried the plug inside of me.

Oh my.

Was he going to fuck me now? Was that what he

had planned. I waited, mute, blind, and deaf, for whatever Dylan had planned next. I waited, and then I felt him move. He left me there for quite a while before he came back with dry hands. He must have washed them, because they weren't as oily now. Most of the oil had absorbed into my skin, so I could tell when he touched my ass that his hands were clean.

He sat in the position he'd been in before and spread my legs. Totally cut off from the world, his invasive use of my body seemed almost clinical, but at the same time, his touch excited me. My eyes moved behind the blindfold, but this one cut off all light, so I couldn't even see shadows.

What was coming next? I was at the point of misbehaving, but a light slap to my ass calmed me down. It also did delightful things to the plug in my ass. How did he always know when I was at that point? Could he feel my tension?

After the slap on my ass, his hands moved between my legs, and I felt something clamp tightly onto my clitoris. My legs went tense. Oh no. Not that again. Fuck...

I moaned as suction mixed with vibration suddenly, and I nearly lost my mind. His hands came up underneath me, and two of the same contraptions were clamped down over my nipples before he turned me to my stomach. A round pillow was slid between my lower abdomen and the mat to tilt my hips up, and my face pressed deeper into the mat.

"Fuck," I muttered around the ball, but he didn't respond.

The suction increased on my clit, as did the vibration around it, and my hips started to move. For a moment, I wondered if Dylan was filming this, but that wasn't in our contract so I knew he wouldn't. He wanted a good angle of my physical reaction to all of this.

When a dildo probed at my vaginal opening, I nearly cried. Yeah, he was going to take this pretty far tonight. This wasn't just a way to get me off, it was going to be many, many orgasms. He was going to make me come over and over again, until I couldn't even lift my head. My clit would vibrate for days after, and my nipples would too.

Not to mention how much it wore me out.

Dylan began to move the dildo inside of me, that combined with the pressure in my ass, and the contraptions all over me, and I was off like a rocket. My body tensed and I came hard, as Dylan watched me. He slapped my ass as the first wave began to ebb, and that sent me off again. He did it again, harder, and then even harder, and I came all over again. I came so many times I lost count. I came so many times I felt almost hysterical and began to cry.

I couldn't even sob out my exhaustion, my

"doneness", by the time he pulled everything out and off of me. When he took me to the shower, all I could do was hiccup and let him wash me. I didn't know what he might have gained from the experience, because he didn't actually fuck me. He just made me come. He hadn't got off at all.

I was very confused and feeling upset, but I was too tired, too drained to say anything. I'd do it tomorrow, I decided. Tomorrow, I'd tell him to tone it down a notch or two. That was too much for me.

He cleaned me from head to toe, and even dried my hair with the hair dryer, before he took me into what I'd come to think of as our bedroom. He put a pair of soft pajamas on me, and then put me under the duvet on our bed. He left me for a moment and came back with a glass of apple juice.

I drank it and thanked him before I turned over and faced away from him. I just wanted to sleep, to get rid of this exhaustion. Dylan curled in behind me, but he wasn't quiet. Not at all.

8

DYLAN

"My childhood wasn't very nice," I heard him say behind me. I stayed still, afraid that if I moved, he'd stop talking. "You know that already, don't you, my sweet little darling?"

I shifted my head just enough to let him know I was listening. I did not want to interrupt what might prove to be a flood of revelations. I'd known something was on his mind. I'd even suspected that part of his life was part of it, but I wouldn't push him. Dylan wasn't the kind who would respond to that very well.

"My mother was schizophrenic, from what I can gather. I don't know a whole lot about her condition really. She wasn't very trustful of doctors, and psychiatrists and psychologists were just quacks, as far as she was concerned. She knew she had problems, she knew she should take medicines, but that wasn't good enough for her. In her mind, there was absolutely nothing wrong with her."

He took a breath, and I turned around to comfort him. My hand splayed over his flat stomach, but it wasn't to entice; it was to let him know he wasn't alone.

His next breath was a little shaky, but he got it in and continued.

"She..." he paused, and I could feel the way his jaw worked as he fought to find a way to make it all make sense to me. "She'd deliberately got pregnant with me to trap my father. He had a good job, he was handsome, and she wanted to have a nice life. So she got pregnant on purpose."

I wanted to say, *but that never works out well*, or *that wasn't your fault*, but I held back. I just stroked his stomach with the flat of my fingers and waited for him to get it all out. I'd seen the newspaper clippings and websites dedicated to murderers and their crimes that had featured the story. This wasn't news to me, but Dylan's side of it was, and I didn't want to stop that for anything.

"My father, a steady worker, a kind man, and dedicated to his family, was patient with her. He didn't care that she'd trapped him. He wanted a family, and he loved her. He hadn't seen her really crazy side yet, but he would. As her pregnancy progressed and her hormones stormed around inside her body, she went bat-shit crazy. At one point she tried to stab herself, and me, but he managed to stop her."

Again, he paused, gathered his thoughts, and then carried on. "They were both alone. Her father had never been around, and her mom was murdered when my mother was fifteen. Dad's parents died in a car accident, and that's what had initially held them together. They wanted what they'd never actually had, a real family."

This time, he leaned over to the nightstand and took a drink from the glass of water there. "It's coming out all messy. I'm sorry about that, but I haven't talked about this since I was a teenager. It's all jumbled around in my head. The main point is my dad tried so hard to make her happy, he did everything he could have possibly done, but he wouldn't demand she be committed, even when he should have. He couldn't let her go to one of those places, especially when he saw documentaries about how terrible those places had been."

I made a noise, not a word, just a noise, and moved so that I could look up at him, but my hand was still on his stomach. I felt like that hand was an anchor between us. It kept us both calm, and I didn't want to move it.

"For years, he dealt with the scenes she'd cause. He'd hold her when she wanted to run, he'd lock himself in their bedroom with her when she wanted to slice her wrists, or swallow a bunch of aspirin. He'd chase her down when she wandered out into the woods with nothing on in the middle of winter. He'd talk to her so softly, and he'd tell her he loved her, over and over, that it didn't matter, that nothing mattered but her and me."

What it must have been like for him, as he witnessed all this, squeezed my heart so hard I felt as if I'd forgotten how to breathe. A kid, with those big gray eyes of his and that mop of dark hair, just sitting there watching his mother go more and more mad, as his father did what he thought was best to protect her.

I couldn't hold the image because I'd start to cry, and he didn't need that right now. How different our childhoods had been. Mine had been cold, maybe full of burdens, but nothing like ... his. Fuck.

"In between all of that, my father took care of me. He fed me, washed my clothes, and made sure I was clean before I went to school. He made me birthday cakes and bought me Christmas presents. He mended my clothes when I'd mess them up. He took me to the doctor and on school trips. At the same time, he kept working, providing, and he must have been one very tired man, but he never complained. He just kept on loving us."

He looked down at me, and for a moment he

smiled. "You're so pretty, Emily, do you know that?"

I could see that tender Dylan again, the one from the cabin, and my heart fluttered. I smiled back at him, and he repositioned his head on the arms he'd placed behind his head.

"She'd often try to take out her rages on me, but Dad would always keep her away from me. She'd become obsessed with this idea that she'd ruined my father's life and that I had ruined hers. She'd done everything on purpose, but somehow it was my fault that her life had changed. I hadn't asked her to birth me, and I certainly didn't have a say in the matter, but that's how she thought. Eventually, she came to the conclusion that if she killed me, my father would be free of both of us. That's when Dad really should have had her put away."

Fucking hell, I thought, surely his Dad hadn't made him live with her then?

"I'd wake up at night and hear her raving at the walls."

Fuck, his dad had made him live through that then. Dammit, man, what were you thinking? I didn't say it. I just kept quiet. He started to stroke my hand that had gone still on his stomach, and I started to stroke him again.

"I like that, keep doing it."

I kissed his shoulder and stroked away.

"So yeah, she started really going bonkers about

the time I turned thirteen. She'd always had this thing where she'd break every dish in the house and scream the night away, but it turned into her trying to bang her way through the walls so she could get at me. Dad would hold her down on their bed, just to keep her from destroying the house. He'd force a sleeping pill down her mouth, and the house would go quiet, but I always wondered if she'd ever wake up without him knowing. I doubt he actually slept at all that last year."

Another shaky breath and Dylan carried on.

"She'd been so bad about breaking dishes that we only had plastic bowls, cups, and plates in the house. Even the cutlery was plastic after a while. She'd destroyed every picture frame, statue, and house plant he'd ever put into the house. Paintings would be ripped to shreds, and vases would just become projectiles. He brought her home flowers often, but when he caught her using the damn things to beat me, he stopped buying them for her."

"Jesus, Dylan!" I couldn't help that, but thankfully he didn't stop. He needed to tell me this, and so much of his life now makes sense, but I'd think about all of that later. For now, I listened.

"She wasn't always bad, though. Sometimes she'd smile at me, make me a sandwich, or cut my hair. Sometimes she'd tell him how much she loved him, and how he was the only thing that mattered to her. She really did love him. Me? I still don't know. Her actions said otherwise, but then, she wasn't sane, was she?" He swiped at his face, then put his hand back behind his head.

"She'd have these phases where she'd look okay for a few days, maybe even weeks sometimes, and then, it would be screaming fits every night, rage that would make her break things during the day, and then more screaming at night. We lived out in the country, and Dad had learned being anywhere near neighbors was a bad idea, although we had a few about half a mile up the road. They came that night…"

His entire body shivered, and I just held him close.

"She'd been really bad, worse than normal, and Dad had sent me to bed to try to deal with her. Seeing me made it worse, and I'd learned to hide in my room to keep her calm. I'd even climb into my bedroom window sometimes, so she wouldn't see me come home from school. Dad never said anything about it, but he somehow knew when I was home. He probably heard the school bus drop me off, now that I think about it." He kind of laughed a little, but there was still a dark note to it.

"That last night she'd been raging, accusing him of cheating, even though he didn't have time for an affair. The furthest Dad had ever gone out of the house at night was to his shed, where he fooled around with HAM radio stuff. Everything went quiet suddenly, and I'd started to think it was over, but I should have known better."

He breathed in and out for a few minutes, before he could go on.

"Dad got her calm, somehow, and I peeked out of the bedroom door. They were on the couch. She turned her head just as I stuck my head out, and I could see that evil in her face. She was calm, but she had something up her sleeve. I decided to read, to try to stay awake, but when she came in my room, I pretended I was asleep."

This time the pause was much longer, and I thought that maybe he wouldn't go on. That he'd come to a point where he couldn't say anything else. I bit my lip, pulled it in between my teeth to keep from saying anything, to stop my impulse to prod him, and stroked his stomach instead.

I started to wonder if he'd fallen asleep and jumped when he started to speak.

"Hours passed, and everything was quiet. I'd seen that threat in her face, that look that always said she was up to something, but Dad must have missed it. And somehow, he'd gone to sleep, but Mom was still awake, but I didn't know that yet. I thought he must have been out in his shed when I realized she was still up. That never happened, Dad going to sleep before her. Dad always made sure she took her pills, because eventually one stopped working and she had to take more, different ones, to get to sleep. But Dad always made sure she was asleep before he went to bed. He must have gotten too complacent, because *she* was awake that night, and he *wasn't*."

Another sip of water and he carried on.

"When she came in to my room, I pretended I'd fallen asleep with the light on. I didn't want her to see my eyes. Something scared me about her that night, and I just wanted her to go away. She didn't leave, though. She came up to me and stroked my hair until I opened my eyes. I didn't say anything, I just watched her. She started to speak."

His voice shook, but he managed to keep going.

"'I've always loved you, baby boy. You gave me your father, but it's time now. It's time to end his infidelity, and to make sure you never leave me either. Sleep well, my boy. Mommy loves you.' That's what she said to me just before she started to pour a gallon of gasoline on the walls of my room and on the floor."

"Fuck … Dylan, stop…" I'd heard the terror in his voice, and I wanted it to stop.

"No, let me go on, Emily. I have to tell you this now, or I may never tell you."

I settled down onto his chest, my hand at his stomach.

"She left the room, and as soon as I heard her go down the hall, I climbed out of my window. The fumes were gagging me, and I was terrified. If she lit that gasoline or if a spark popped off of something, I was dead, so I climbed out and headed for my father's shed. Like I said, he never went to sleep before her, so I thought he was out there. I heard a loud noise, and then the house lit up. I ran to the shed, but Dad wasn't in there, and I knew he must have been in the house. I tried to run back inside, but she must have poured a few dozen gallons of gasoline over the place, because every room was on fire."

He shifted a little, but I had a feeling it was more to do with his story than with how comfortable he was.

"By the time the neighbors came, I was just a puddle on the ground, watching the house burn. I'd run around the house dozens of times, trying to find a way in. I'd screamed until I couldn't scream anymore, and then, I collapsed. I was exhausted, in shock, and totally out of it by the time emergency services arrived. And they were all there: the fire department, an ambulance, and the police. I thought I'd be taken off in the ambulance, because I couldn't speak to anyone, I could only stare. Somehow, insanely, I was put into the back of the policeman's car."

"Why?" I knew why, but I still asked.

"Because I was the loner, the kid who never spoke to anyone, the kid who always wore black. I never caused trouble, but somehow that was ignored. I was weird and quiet, so I must have killed my parents, or so they thought."

"It's all so terrible, Dylan."

"I know, and I know it's not easy to hear. I'm sorry, but I wanted you to know."

"I know the rest. You don't have to tell me anymore, if you don't want to."

"About the trial and my adoptive parents, you mean?" He looked down at me, surprised.

"Yeah, I looked you up when I figured out who you were and after..." I was about to say after Trent called him a murderer but stopped myself.

"You've known all this time?" He looked stunned but pleased.

"Yeah, I did. The past doesn't have to define who you are now, you know, Dylan? I never thought you were bad, or that you must be sick if your mom was, if that's what you're thinking. Other people might be that stupid, but I'm not. You're a man who comes from a shattered past. That might affect who you are now, but it doesn't define you."

"Thank you." He looked at me with wonder in his eyes, and I kissed his jaw.

"I'm sorry that happened to you, Dylan, I really am. Your mother's mother was murdered you said?" I paused to let him nod. "Then she must have had her own demons before your father and her trap ever happened. I think there wasn't anything more you could do, and none of it was your fault."

"Thank you, Emily. Thank you for listening, and still being here."

"Like I said, Dylan, the past doesn't have to define you." I thought about my own past and knew I had my own foibles and problems, but it didn't have to define who I was now. "You're a wonderful person to me, and that's all that matters to me. You are Dylan, and that's all I want you to be."

We settled down together, and the room went dark. I hoped he'd exorcised that demon, or as much as he could from one so old. He had a new life, and he didn't have to let the past change who he was now. He had a new life and a much happier one ahead of him, if he chose to take it.

He'd given me trust beyond anything he ever had before. I had to be very careful not to break it.

9

DYLAN

The next day, I found myself at a restaurant waiting for a designer that I was supposed to have a lunch meeting with. Emily had stayed home, and I was thinking about what had happened the night before. I hadn't exactly planned to dump my trauma on her the way I had, but it had felt like the right time to give her my version of it.

I'd gathered that she'd read about me long before she admitted that she had, and I knew the kind of things she was likely to have read. The gruesome newspaper stories, the flashy websites that promised lurid details not revealed elsewhere, pictures of me and the family for the really curious. It was all available online, and anyone who typed my name into a search engine would find it.

I felt as if I'd lost real weight now, as if telling

her my story had released the burden I'd carried around for so long. And maybe it had, I didn't know yet, but today, there was little that could wipe the smile off of my face.

I looked around the room. The room was simple but elegant. The walls were covered in a dark blue damask pattern, and the tables were covered in white cloths. The chairs were a pretty pine, and the room was pleasing in a non-descript sort of way. It was one of the best restaurants in town, but you'd never guess from the décor.

The designer I wanted to hire for the hotel came to the table, and I stood to greet her. "Hello, Miss Mills."

The woman was in her fifties, but she'd never been married and made no bones about it. She was Miss and nothing more.

"Oh, please call me Erica. I'm not late, am I? I'm new to the area, you know, and get turned around so easily." She settled down and placed a bag in the empty chair at our table.

"No, you aren't late, Erica. What would you like to drink?" I tipped my head to a waiter, and he came to take our orders for drinks.

"I'm happy to be of any help I can be to you, Dylan, but, I've never worked on a hotel before." Erica looked at me, her face unlined and her blonde hair perfectly in place. She was a beautiful, elegant woman, but I didn't notice her in any other way but as the designer I'd wanted to hire.

"That's it, though. You design homes, and I want my hotel here to feel like home. I want people to already have plans for their next visit in place from the moment they arrive. I want them to miss my hotel."

"Ah, intriguing," she said over her glass of white wine. "What colors do you have in mind?"

"Something like this, elegant but muted. Yet, still, somehow exceptional. I don't want neon greens and oranges, or the tired out blue and white, or even that awful khaki color and green that some are using now. I want stylish, but timeless. Classic and beautiful." Like my Emily, the thought ran through my head, and I smiled.

"I see. How many rooms are there?" She leaned in to ask, and we talked for a few minutes.

The waiter came and took our order for lunch, and the conversation carried on. She hadn't been overly confident that she could help me when she first arrived, but I think by the time she stood to leave that she was as convinced as I was. She'd won countless awards for her design skills, and I thought she might just win another for what she would do with my hotel.

I stood when she got ready to leave, or I wouldn't have seen the man from where I sat at the table. He must have been in another room of the restaurant, because if I'd seen him before I'd have arranged to eat somewhere else. Trent Thompson.

Emily's brother.

I bid farewell to Erica and sat back down. I'd have to pay the bill, so I waited and watched Trent. The man didn't look like a demon, just a bastard, but what kind of man would disown his sister as Trent had? Sure, he thought he'd done it for good reasons, but even I knew the man hated me for no other reason than he thought I'd be competition for him. He didn't give two fucks about my past, he just didn't want the competition he knew I'd give him.

The really stupid part was, there was enough people coming to the place to keep us both in business. So, in essence, he'd lost his sister for nothing. He'd thrown her out in the cold and left her with no way to interact with the rest of her family because of a stupid case of instant dislike. He didn't look like a stupid man, but obviously he was, to treat his sister so callously.

From what Emily said, her entire lifetime had been blemished by this man. He'd been a petulant child who didn't want his daddy to have more children, and when his temper tantrums hadn't sent the horrible new siblings away, he'd just been atrocious to them. Or, at least, to Emily. He'd called some kind of truce with his brothers, but she'd just been a servant. How could he treat somebody as sweet as Emily as he had?

Something kind of went clunk inside of me as I looked the man over. He was talking to another man in a black suit like his own, and he wore a cocksure grin. He hadn't noticed me or I was sure he'd have walked out of the place. This was the man who had made Emily's life so incredibly unbearable that she'd run away from her own family. Well, one of them. From what she'd said, they'd all played a part in her departure.

Trent had been the oldest. He should have looked out for his little sister, protected her, and loved her. Instead, she'd grown up not knowing what real love was until the babies had come along from her brothers. Trent should have been a sensible kid and been a protective brother to the younger siblings.

The whole family was fairly messed up, even I could see that. I decided to keep my mouth shut for now and wait. Emily obviously wanted to make amends with some of her family, and she missed the children. I could tell that from the way her face would change when there were children around us. It wasn't necessarily a need to be a mother; it was memories of her nieces and nephews that turned her face sad and made her go quiet.

I wanted to punch the man for a thousand reasons, but I would let it go for now. Emily deserved a chance to get her family back together.

That was something I'd never have the chance to do.

I paid the bill and went back to the resort to look it over. The designer had promised to have some ideas for me soon enough, and I'd go from there. I wanted something spectacular, but not tacky. I went to the main office, a hidden room at the very back of the reception area, and picked up a set of keys. I rode the elevator to the very top floor and went into the penthouse there.

Glass everywhere, and the movers had been in. The kitchen, laundry room, and the bedroom were ready. Good. There was no pool on the top of this building, but I could install a hot tub or something later. For now, I wanted to make this place my own and get out of the one I'd rented. I wanted it to be a surprise for Emily.

I'd ordered paintings for the walls and a few other items that would add decoration. I'd spent the earliest part of my life in bleak, almost empty rooms, and I'd kept the habit when I became an adult. I wanted her to see how much of a change she'd made in my life, and had decided the best way to do that was to ask her to pick out the china pattern I'd buy for the penthouse. I wanted her to have a part in the decoration.

She'd made a liar out of me, and I knew now that the man who didn't do relationships was deep into one he didn't want to end. I knew she was going to be a part of my life for a long time, if I didn't scare her off. I couldn't get enough of waking up to her, or the way her lips tasted after she'd sipped her apple juice. I wanted her to know that now.

Slowly, it had to be slowly, so neither of us would get spooked, but eventually, I thought this could go a lot further than a casual 'we're dating' scenario. I was afraid, I could admit that to myself, because she could totally destroy me if this went much further. At the same time, it was one of the biggest challenges of my life.

I'd even told my parents about her. That had been a shocker for both of us, believe me. I'd never mentioned a female to them before, and I had to laugh now. I bet they thought I was gay. They'd been delighted when I told them about Emily, and so pleased that I was taking that chance.

It felt good to know I had someone to come home to and that they looked forward to meeting. It felt even better to slip into bed with her, mmm, especially when she was warm and asleep. She'd wrap herself around me in total abandon and make me feel like I was the strongest man alive, because she felt safe with me.

It was that, perhaps, that kept me humble. Because, as much as I was afraid of being hurt by her, she was just as afraid that I'd hurt her.

I closed up the penthouse and went down to the car. A call came in, and I answered it.

"Hi, Dylan, sorry to be a bother, but we have a situation out here at the San Diego hotel, and we need you here." I heard the main manager's voice and sighed. This didn't happen frequently, so I knew the manager had only called me as a last resort.

"What's up, Amanda?" I started the car and pulled out of the parking garage as she told me about the issue at hand. She was right, I'd need to go out there and sort it.

"I'll fly out tomorrow. It can wait until then. Thanks for contacting me, Amanda. I have every confidence in your decision-making abilities, but this needs my attention. I'll see you tomorrow."

She said goodbye with relief in her voice, and I had to shake my head. I didn't see much point in terrorizing my employees, as I'd hired them for a reason. Amanda was more than capable, and I hadn't lied, I was confident in her. Otherwise, she wouldn't have had the position.

I made my way home to Emily at last. She wasn't happy that I'd be leaving again so soon, but she understood. I took her to bed, and she decided to forgive me after I'd made her come a few times with my tongue.

It was later, as we prepared my luggage

together, that I finally asked her the question that had been on my mind.

"Emily, will you move into the new place with me?" I turned to look at her and saw surprise on her face.

"What else would I do, Dylan?" She moved up to me and put her arms around my waist. "You wanted me here. I took it for granted you'd want me there too."

"No, I mean really move in with me. As in, let your old place go and plan to stay for a while?" I felt a little nervous, because this baby step felt like a giant leap.

"Alright." She gave me a calm smile, and her eyes looked up at me with happiness.

"That's all I get, alright? Sheesh, woman!" I hugged her close, happy despite the lack of screeching joy.

"Well, I live with you already. It's just to a new place, right?" She pulled back to look at me again.

"No. I want ... well, I want you to choose the china, the extra little touches, you know, the things that make a place a home?" I watched her until realization dawned. When it did, her eyes went round.

"Oh. Dylan!" She hugged me, and I breathed in relief. At last she got it. I wanted a home, not just a place to live.

This was a new step for both of us. I thought Emily was more prepared for those steps than I was, but she wasn't the kind to push someone into a decision. Unless that decision concerned her own life. She'd pushed me to go beyond a contract, and for a while, I fought against it. Now, I was glad she had. She fought for what she'd wanted, for what she thought was right, and it was one more thing that assured me she was on my side in all things. I could trust her.

We went back to packing my bags, and when we turned the lights off and went to bed, I thought about how much my life had changed because of her. I would miss her over the next few days, and that made me pull her closer. I had an early flight, but I didn't care. I needed her again.

She climbed over me eagerly and took me deep inside the best pussy I've ever slid into. It was no contest. If I could only ever fuck one person on earth again, it would be Emily. The way her walls clenched around me, pulled me deeper inside, was something incredible that I didn't want to give up. That wasn't the only reason I wanted Emily in my life. It was a very distracting reason, though, and when she tilted her head back and really started to grind down on me, I lost all train of thought. There was only Emily, and that was all that mattered.

EMILY

I'd wanted to go to San Diego with Dylan, but he'd told me he'd be busy the entire time he was there and didn't want to leave me sitting in a hotel without him there to take me around. I knew he was right. I wouldn't really want to go see the sights without him, but it would have been better than being here, bored silly.

I tapped my nails on the kitchen table and decided to go out. I called Roxie, and she wasn't busy, so we went out to have our nails done, our usual ritual. When I picked her up and she got in the car, my frown turned upside down, as silly as that sounded.

"You just make me smile, do you know that?" I leaned over and bumped my head near hers. We shared an intimacy I'd never experienced with another female, not even Jesse. A sisterly intimacy, and I knew we'd be friends for life. She'd be there for me, no matter what, or who came along.

"Girl, you know I love you. Come on now, let's get this done and over with. You know I hate those drill things they use." Roxie shivered but smiled at me and gave me a wink.

We spent the day giggling and talking about how life was for each of us. I ended up buying more of those panties that Dylan liked so much, a few pairs in different colors, as well as some other things he'd get to tear off me when he got home.

"I'm so glad things are working out for you, Emily. I was kind of nervous about it all, but something told me you two needed each other," she said as we both gobbled down salads smothered in ranch dressing and ham bits. It was one of my favorite indulgences, even if salad was meant to be a nutritional food.

"I guess you were right, Roxie. He's changed my world, and I think I've started to change his. He asked me to pick out the china for his new place!" She looked at me oddly, and I wanted to explain why that was so important, but that was Dylan's story to tell. So I settled for the ordinary reasons. "It means he wants me to be part of his life in the future, Rox…"

"Ohhhh!" She grinned, and her eyes went wide. "That is a good thing then!"

"It is." I took a deep breath and stared out at the

beach beyond the glass. It was winter now, too rainy and cold to sit outside, but it was still nice to watch the waves coming in. "I think I love him, but I'm afraid to, you know?"

"That's understandable, under the circumstances. He's your first, Emily." She reached out, her hand over mine. "Dylan's something special, I think. You can't let that go because of fear."

She paused and looked away for a moment, as if to decide something. I could see she made her mind up, and she began to speak again.

"We've had different lives, Ems, and you might have had a privileged life, but from where I sit, I sometimes think, despite the shit I dealt with, that I had the better life. I wasn't sold a lie. You were. Then they tried to take a future away from you. You have the chance to take that back with both fists. You need to cling to it, keep it close to yourself, until you know what life is about. You deserve that, girl."

"I understand." I wasn't mad, which was what I guessed she'd been worried about, but Roxie had always been blunt with me. It wasn't cruelty; it was her way of saying she cared.

"You want to watch movies and eat ice cream with me tonight?" I asked, knowing I'd be alone tonight too. Poor Dylan was in some kind of mess out there in California, so I'd left him to deal with it.

"I would like that."

"Wow? Really?" I was excited, she usually said she had to work.

"Yeah, I've decided to take a night off. Fuck 'em, they can handle shit without me."

I got an idea when she said that. The stores had bombarded us for ages now with Christmas music and decorations, even the restaurant had a tree up, while our apartment was bare. I'd already decided to let mine go and would clear it out once Dylan's new place was ready, our new place, but that would be weeks from now.

"Let's go to the store first," I said with a wicked grin, and she looked at me.

"What have you got planned now, my dear?"

"You'll see. Come on, hurry up." We paid our bill and left, and then I drove us to another store.

We nearly cleaned the place out of Christmas decorations, and it took some doing, but we got a Christmas tree in the car and managed to get it up to the apartment with the help of a security guard from downstairs. We both giggled when we got in and started to unpack bags and boxes.

"Are you sure Dylan won't mind?" Roxie asked as she hung some silver decorations on the tree.

"I don't know," I said and paused as I hung a wreath on the wall with a removable hanger. "He's not religious, but he hasn't said he hates Christmas or anything."

"Hmm. I know this much, if my partner had gone through this much trouble to surprise me, I would not complain." She went back to hanging ornaments, and I tried not to laugh.

We had so many lights on the tree, I thought we could act as a beacon for airplanes, but it was pretty, and later, when we turned the lights off, the living room looked like a Christmas wonderland. I even had a tiny little Christmas village on a side table.

"Oh, it's so pretty!" I whispered. When I was young, my parents paid someone to decorate our house for Christmas, and I'd never had the chance to decorate a tree or a house of my own. Later, wherever I went was home, and I was never invited for the decorating or things like that. So this was the first time I'd ever decorated a tree, and I was proud of it. I couldn't wait for Dylan to see it.

He'd either hate it, or he'd love that I'd done it. I had a feeling it would be the latter. He always went to an effort to thank me when I did something for him, which was often. Roxie and I settled down to watch movies and eat ice cream, as we'd planned, and it was fun. We didn't do it often enough.

I broke out a bottle of wine, and we watched some more movies. Before long, she was asleep on the couch, and I left her there. I went into the kitchen and hung up the kitchen towels I'd bought, and set a plate down on the counter. It was the pattern I'd chosen for our new place.

Maybe it was a bit old fashioned, but I'd loved the rose petals and the gold edging. It was maybe even a little tacky, not modern at all, but I wanted something that expressed my tastes in that place, something that said I lived there too. I wanted something that was different, colorful, so I'd chosen the pattern.

Dylan would accept it, because I wanted it, and I smiled because I was confident in him now. We might not be quite at the stage where we were planning our wedding or picking out baby names, but we were both making an attempt at being grownups with real relationships.

I sat in the kitchen and realized just how lucky I was. Things might not have been completely solid with Dylan, but they were as solid as they could be, and in the living room I had a real friend. One who wanted what was best for me, not what she thought I wanted to hear so that I'd just shut up and watch her kids. Which might be a little unfair to my sisters-in-law. They were so enamored with their husbands, kids, and lives that I was just a background, no different to other people in their lives.

I kind of envied that kind of love. It was something I wanted with Dylan, and I had to admit, he consumed my thoughts now. For once, I didn't feel bad about that. He was truly amazing to me, and he deserved the love I could give him. He'd allowed his adoptive parents to love him, but he hadn't let anyone else into his life. Until me.

I had to make sure I continued to deserve that chance. I'd nearly messed it up when I didn't tell him who I was before he found out. The second I'd walked out the door I'd felt the world begin to collapse. Then he'd come after me, and there'd been a pause in that destruction. Then we went to the mountains, and he'd given me snow.

Then there'd been a few dark days, when I'd started to worry about him, but he'd worked it out, and now we were closer than ever. That wasn't a bad thing.

I got up, walked into the glow of the living room, and wondered if I'd gone overboard. I was certain I had, but oh well. It was my first Christmas on my own. I could go a little wild, surely? I turned the lights off, covered Roxie up, and touched her cheek. She had given me so much, and it touched me how she'd fallen asleep so quickly. She'd had it rough lately, and she'd been working her ass off, obviously. She'd still be awake normally, so at least I could give her some rest.

I went to the bedroom and scrolled around online, looking for a Christmas present for Dylan. I wanted something that would make him smile. What could it be? He wasn't a gaming console kind of guy, he was too busy to play games. The only jewelry he'd ever worn was the jewelry I bought him.

Hmmm. I did a search for gifts for men, but everybody thought their products made great gifts for men. I didn't think plumbing pipes were that great of a gift, but a woman selling handmade knitted sweaters caught my eye. I found a few things in her online shop that I liked. A gray cable-knit sweater, some gloves, and a hat in the same yarn, all went into my basket.

I could give him a hug for hours in that sweater, I thought with a goofy grin. Or at least give him the feeling of being hugged, which was corny, but fuck it. They weren't cheap presents, and I paid extra for quick delivery. I found a few other things that I liked on other shops and bought those too. Soon, I'd have presents to go under the tree.

I felt almost like a kid again, only this time, the big kid was able to really act on her instincts. When I was younger I always had to be so proper, I was never allowed to misbehave, and after a while, it never occurred to me. When other girls were going bad and acting wild, I stayed at home and did whatever was needed of me. Maybe part of me felt a little guilty about Trent, that he'd lost his real mother and he'd had to deal with us. For a long time I felt like I owed him more because of that. Now? He could fuck off.

I'd paid him back a thousand times for what

he'd lost, and for real, he could have seen us as gifts, but he'd just pouted. Now? Well? I might have had an extra glass of wine to prove that I could do what I wanted to. I was a grown fucker, I'd do what I'd want.

I laughed loudly, but smothered it when I remembered Roxie was in the living room. I put some Enrique Iglesias on my phone, plugged in my earbuds, and began to dance around my bedroom like a lunatic. Can you blame me? I was one happy woman and had a lot to look forward to. For the first time in my life, I was truly free and almost wild.

I had given up an entire family, for one man, but I was getting far more from the deal than that. I got my freedom, I got to be me, even if I was only learning who that was now. I had a lot to be happy about, and some dancing seemed to be in order for the occasion.

DYLAN

I arrived at the penthouse ready to tear Emily's clothes off and fuck her until neither of us could hold our heads up. I'd made a stop in Kansas to pick up some test results, and I hadn't really wanted to spend too much time thinking about what the doc said, so I'd fantasized about her the whole way back on the plane. I was more than ready for her when the elevator doors opened on my floor.

Maybe I should have called her to let her know I'd be home today. I wasn't sure how long I was going to spend in Kansas, and I hadn't wanted to tell her about that trip. As a result, my coming home was a surprise. As soon as I opened the door, I knew I should have called her.

The whole place smelled like a Christmas

extravaganza of gingerbread cookies and peppermint candy. When I made it out of the hallway I found out why. I was completely shocked to find the living room a Christmas wonderland, right down to a very large tree filled to the brim with decorations.

I walked into the kitchen and then the bathroom and found those had been decorated too. Even our bed had winter-themed sheets and a comforter on them. I grinned as I thought about how she must have worked really hard to get all of this done. It was almost too much, but I could see the childlike enthusiasm that had gone into it. This was a person who had finally been allowed to do just as she'd pleased when it came to Christmas decorations, and she'd done it well.

The overall affect was a tad overwhelming, but at the same time, it invited you to come in and play, to join in the festivities with total abandon. An idea formed as I walked back into the living room. Emily had a degree in hotel management, and she'd never had the chance to use it. Even her family didn't know she'd managed to rack up that accomplishment. I wondered how she'd feel about working for me.

She was a smart woman, sensible in most things, and dedicated to the causes she took up. She would be an asset to any company that wanted to succeed. I'd get to see her when I was at the hotel working.

The more I thought about it the more I liked the idea, and I decided I'd ask her when she made it home. I also knew I should go out and pretend she'd surprised me.

I picked up everything I'd dropped off and made my way out to a shopping center. I picked a few things, and then I went to have something to eat. I texted her and waited for her response.

When I got a reply, I smiled. She was more than a little happy to find out I was home and said she was on her way back to the penthouse. I was given strict orders to wait for her to be home before I made my way up. I knew then that she wanted to surprise me, and I'd been right to come out.

I thought about what she'd done and how excited she was and thought about past Christmases. When I was little, we couldn't have a tree. The one time Dad had tried to put one up, Mom had almost torched the house when she tried to put candles on the thing for some reason. Dad put lights on it, but she'd wanted the candles anyway.

When I was older and had gone to live with the James family, they'd always put up a tree and decorated, but there was always something restrained about their Christmas displays. They weren't religious people, and I thought the only reason they even celebrated Christmas was because of me. I'd appreciated their efforts and would always love that they'd tried, but what Emily had produced with very little space really impressed me.

I waited about twenty minutes then made the drive to the penthouse. When I texted her that I was home, she came down in the elevator to meet me. She looked happy but nervous. We'd never really talked much about religion or holidays, and I knew she was probably worried about how I'd react.

"I've got a surprise for you, Dylan," she said after we'd made our way to the elevator to go up. I had her tucked up under my arm, and her left arm was wrapped around my back. I really wanted to pin her to the wall and have my way with her, but I knew this was important to her, so I tried to stay sane for a few more minutes. For her sake.

"Have you, indeed, princess?" I kissed the top of her head and brought her around to face me. "What is it?"

"Well, I've, uh…" She had the cutest face when she was excited but uncertain about something. Like a naughty child who wanted you to be pleased with their exploits but wasn't sure you should be.

"You've what?" I lifted an eyebrow as I stared down and gave her a look that said I was curious.

"I've, well, you'll just have to wait and see." I guessed she lost her nerve because she moved away and stared at the numbers on the panel.

"Hmm. Is this going to be something that deserves a spanking, by any chance?" I teased as I bent down to whisper in her ear. "I've missed you terribly and can't wait to have you riding my dick, Emily."

"Dylan!" she said and turned to me, her eyes wide. Then this little smirk came, and I knew she wasn't as shocked as she pretended to be. Or wanted to, whichever was the case. "No, it shouldn't deserve a spanking."

Her tiny little nose went up in the air, and she side-eyed me, but I could see the way her lips twitched.

"Are you sure?" I tried to pull her back, but she slapped my hands away and stared up at the ceiling in mock annoyance.

"I am quite sure." She even nodded for emphasis. Minx.

"Hmm. I guess we'll find out now." I took her hand as the elevator came to a stop, and we stepped through the penthouse door together.

"Oh my, what's that smell?" I asked as I sat down my bags and luggage. "Did you make cookies? Is that my surprise?"

"No! Come with me." Her eyes danced with joy now, and she was the one who pulled as I followed her into the living room.

I let the wonder of it all come over me again

and examined every aspect of her decorations a second time. "I love it!"

"Do you?" She almost danced in place as she watched me. I nodded and looked around.

"It's like the Christmas I always wanted but never had," I declared and meant it. It was every kid's fantasy of what a home should look like for Christmas.

"I know we didn't talk about it, but it's not far away now, and well, I couldn't help it. I was out with Roxie, and we kind of went overboard with the decorations."

"Did you leave any in the store?" I asked as I walked into the kitchen to get a drink.

"I left a few. I didn't want to be too greedy." I saw the pleased smile she tried to hide behind her hands and pulled her into my arms.

"I love it, Emily. It's perfect, really. Just like you." She was to me. Every inch of her was pure perfection. "Can I get you naked now?"

"May I?" she said primly and pulled away. "No, not yet. I need a shower, and then maybe you can. I've been out all day."

It wasn't late, but it had gone dark. She wasn't usually out that late, unless it was for her charity, so I didn't begrudge her a shower. I could use one myself, but I waited for her to finish before I went in. When I came out a little while later, she was in a very sultry long, gray nightgown that matched my eyes more than hers.

The material was silky, and soft black lace trimmed the neckline and hem. She'd made two cups of coffee, set out a few snacks, and was curled up on the couch waiting for me when I came in.

"Sit with me, tell me how the trip went." She held her hand out, and I took it before I sat beside her.

"It went fine." I pushed the doctor's words to the back of mind and focused on the first part of my trip. "I got the problem sorted out quickly enough and put steps in place so that the hotel manager could deal with those kinds of problems in the future. She'll still have to consult me, but I won't have to fly out there next time something similar happens. Because there's always a next time."

"Good. I hated you being gone so long." She leaned against the arm of the couch, and the lights from the Christmas tree illuminated her in a way I found rather magical.

Thoughts left my head, and I stared at her like a love-struck schoolboy who was in the throes of his first crush. She was just ... beautiful.

"You know, you amaze me, Emily. You really do."

"Why do you say that?" she asked with a confused look.

"You just carry on, no matter what life throws at

you. I know it must be hard for you right now, being without your family, but you just smile anyway and make the best of it."

"It's not like I could do anything else." She looked more perplexed than confused now, but it settled into a smile. "Besides, it's hard to be sad when you've come home."

Home. She'd called this place home. I looked away and made myself busy picking up a strawberry. I didn't want her to see my face because I probably looked like some goofy kid.

The news from the doctor had been … alright. The new medicine had started to work at last, and as long as it kept that up, I'd be fine. He did warn me that if anything happened, more symptoms, or something became worse, that I was to come right back and see him. If it was bad enough, he'd said, I should go to the emergency room. That was the part that worried me, that I could develop a symptom so bad I'd need emergency care.

I tried to push the thought away. I was young, mostly healthy, and kept away from cigarettes and food that was far from healthy. I kept in shape and exercised often. I was happy for the first time in my life, really happy, and had a woman who could change the entire world for me. The fact that this was happening now, when life had suddenly become good for me, really pissed me off.

I wouldn't think about it, I reminded myself. I

sat back against the couch with Emily and sighed. There was no need to rush to bed, I decided, as she turned the television on and found a movie for us to watch. I had time to do all the things I'd fantasized about and then some.

She fell asleep curled up in my lap not long before the movie ended. I could have woken her up and taken her to bed, but the thought struck me that this was trust. She was totally unguarded, without any kind of protection at all, but she still fell asleep. That meant she felt safe with me, and I wasn't sure I'd ever made anyone feel safe before in my life. Only her. She trusted me to keep her safe, and she trusted me to not harm her.

She was totally unconcerned about what might happen to her, and that really hit me hard. She'd fallen asleep on me before, but it hadn't really occurred to me what that meant. She trusted me implicitly.

I knew I should tell her what was wrong with me. She'd have to know if our relationship went on any longer, but for now, I wanted to keep it a secret. Was my failure to tell her a form of dishonesty? It wasn't something she could catch from me, it wasn't something like that, but it would impact my health and my way of life, eventually. I would have to tell her before the day came when I'd need help.

I didn't want her to think of me as a patient,

though, or to burden her with that knowledge, not right now. If, and when, the day came that I'd need more care than I needed right now, I'd tell her. It would be her choice to make about whether she stayed with me.

I didn't really have much concern about that either, if I was honest. I knew how loyal she was and knew she wouldn't leave me just because of an illness. I didn't want her to stay because of that loyalty, however. I shifted as guilt started to nag at me.

I shouldn't have started this relationship, not with such an uncertain future ahead of me, but Emily was a storm wrapped in a blessing that I hadn't counted on. She'd thrown everything inside of me into havoc, while she made everything outside seem calm and sensible. She gave me hope that I could have a future, and I loathed to give that up now.

I brushed at her cheek softly as she began to snore and smile. Even her snores were soft and unobtrusive. I reached for my phone, made sure it was in silent mode, and then took a picture of her there, on my lap, completely angelic looking.

She'd hate it if she knew I'd taken that picture, but I knew it was one I'd look at often in the future. I had a few of her, and I'd look at them every night before I went to sleep while I was away. We would do video chats, and we talked every day, but I still liked to see these moments we'd captured together before I went to sleep without her. Sometimes the life she'd given me in our short time together seemed unreal. I'd take out the pictures, have a look at them, and know that it wasn't all a fantasy. Emily was mine, she was real, and I'd do whatever it took to keep it that way.

12

EMILY

I woke up the next morning and prepared some breakfast for both of us. I knew he liked light breakfasts, I did too, so it wasn't too complicated. I'd learned to cook from my brother Trent's wife when we were both young. I thought about her now, and the hurt that came with thoughts of my family dimmed my happy expression.

Dylan made the hurt disappear the instant he walked into the kitchen and slid his arms around me from behind. "Good morning, Emily. Have I said how much I love this Christmas wonderland you've created?"

"You have, but thank you. I really like it, and I'm glad you do too." I drizzled a little icing onto the cherry-filled pastries I'd baked and brought the plate to the small table we sat at in the mornings. "Come eat before they get cold."

"Fine." He dragged the word out like a teenager that had been asked to clear the dishwasher, but smiled as he sat. "You know these are my favorite, right?"

"I do, indeed." I picked one up and carefully bit into the flaky pastry. The taste was heavenly, I had to admit.

"What are you going to do today?" he asked after he swallowed a bite of his food and then watched me.

"I have no plans, actually." I didn't want to admit it, but I was starting to get bored sitting at home all day on my own. There were enough books in the world to keep me occupied for the rest of my life, but I liked to be active too.

"How about you come into work with me then?" he asked, and I felt excitement bubble to life.

"Really?" I took another bite and waited.

"Yes. You have a good eye for decoration, and I'd like your input on a few things." He didn't quite meet my eye, but I understood. He was busy eating.

"Oh. Thanks." I felt heat bloom in my cheeks and looked down at the last bite of my pastry. I was pleased that he thought that.

"I'm going to get dressed, just casual stuff for now. We don't even have furniture in the place yet, so there's no need for anything more."

"Great. I'll join you then." The bathroom had enough room to accommodate both of us, so we showered and dressed together, and managed to get through it without too many distractions. Although, before we left the house, he pinned me to the wall in the hallway and kissed me absolutely silly.

His tongue swirled around mine for a long moment as his hand went to my waist. I had on a pair of jeans and a long gray sweater with a pair of designer combat boots on my feet. A long gray scarf finished off the look, but instead of letting it warm my neck, he was pulling it off to wrap around my waist. When he pulled tightly to him with the scarf, I moaned into his mouth.

Dylan, the bastard, pulled his mouth from mine, and I tried to follow, but he stood up straight, smirked that infuriatingly adorable smile of his, and ran his finger through his hair to straighten the mess my hands had made of it.

"Let's get out of here before I take you back to the bedroom and remove that rather concealing sweater you have on."

I was in a daze by the time he put my scarf around my neck and pulled me into the elevator. I swear, I heard him chuckle when he started the car, and I looked over to give him a glare, but his face was clear of any kind of chuckling activity.

"You know you make my brain go dead when

you kiss me like that," I complained at him, and he chuckled out loud.

"Of course, I know that. Why else would I do it?"

My muttered response was drowned out by the sound of the engine of the car as he pulled into traffic, and I let it all go with a contented smile. It wasn't like I was going to complain too hard about being kissed silly. It was a wonderful thing.

Dylan drove us toward the beachfront, and I was surprised when he pulled into the parking garage. My family's resort wasn't far from this one, and I'd heard Trent say more than once that he'd like to acquire it, but the owner refused all of his offers. I wondered how Dylan had managed it but didn't ask. It was none of my business.

"This, my lovely, will be the newest version of Pebbles, my own brand of resorts." He guided me into another elevator that soon opened into the lobby. "There are seven floors of rooms, four penthouse suites, one of which will be ours, and a few rooms that we will use for staff quarters, should the need arise."

He guided me into the reception area, and I could see workers had already gutted most of the furnishings and the carpets. Cement and drywall waited to be painted or covered by paneling. The reception was located at the rear of the building, opposite the beachfront side. That made it convenient to the parking garage, but I wondered if a separate office would be useful on the side that faced the beach.

"There is space for a bar inside, an infinity pool, which so many families want now, a bar at the back, and two restaurants." I watched him, this normally confident man who now seemed uncertain, nervous even.

"It's a good place to start. Definitely a good place to start. It's in a good location; you're on the beach. How many pools are there?" I was thinking about possibilities, and already my brain had returned to the old days of maintaining a resort from the back end, the part that none of my brothers had ever wanted to deal with.

"There are three pools and several hot tubs. We have plenty of water activities. I'm planning to put a full gym in, one of the bars will probably end up an Internet café type of area, and I have other ideas." His words trailed off as his thoughts spun out to the future.

I could see what he wanted, a place where the guests never had to leave and families could spend their days together. "Have you thought about shuttle services, for those who want to see the sights?"

"I have, and I'm scouting a fleet now. I've also got someone working on how many staff we'll need. Most of that is coming from my dad's resorts.

I'll be able to put a lot of the practices from there into place here. I'll pull in some of my staff from California for a little while until the staff here is trained properly. It's a huge task, but I think it's manageable."

"You can do it, Dylan. I know you can." I walked around the bare space and wondered at the possibilities. I didn't want to butt in and give too many opinions.

Dylan was as deep into hotel management as I was, and he didn't need my two cents to add into the pot of advice I was sure he was already getting. I walked around and couldn't help but add in my own touches. I'd put a plant there, to hide the odd corner, and a chair in case someone wanted a corner to sit in if lines got long at reception.

In fact, I'd put a couch or two in here, and a table for a laptop and drinks that always came with large crowds. I couldn't help but start to problem-solve for Dylan the same as I'd done in my family's hotels around the world.

"I can't believe I've spent so much time in hotels," I said with a laugh. I'd told Dylan about my childhood, and then the adult years, so many endless days in hotels, dealing with problems. When my brothers were old enough to cause problems, I was called in a lot of the time to deal with it until my father got back.

Even as a teenager, I was the one who made

decisions about what was to be done, how to control the damage. I'd been a problem-solver my entire life it would seem. I could do that for Dylan too.

I brushed the thought away as nonsense. Dylan has just said he was bringing staff in from his other resorts. He didn't need me one bit.

He took me through the rest of the hotel and then we went home to have some lunch. Dylan had a meeting with a designer, but he told me he'd be back around five to take me to dinner. He'd been so nervous and almost twitchy that I'd been worried about him.

When he returned, I met him in the parking garage. He seemed calmer, if somewhat quiet. It wasn't long before we arrived at one of our favorite restaurants and had placed our orders.

"Emily, I have an offer for you," Dylan said from his seat across the table.

We always had the same table, in a private nook of the dining area, away from prying eyes. I was distracted, my mind on whether or not I should run my foot up his thigh, when he made his announcement.

My head tilted as I grew curious. "What's that, Dylan? You want me to crawl under the tablecloth and open your zipper for you?"

It never failed to amaze me how aroused I always was around him. I was only half-teasing.

The thought of doing just what I'd said made me flush, and something odd happened to my breathing.

He leaned across the table, placed his hand over mine, and looked me right in the eye. I knew the offer had turned his mind from whatever he was about to say because his gaze turned hot, and his lips turned that shade of red that only came when he was aroused. My eyes narrowed when he licked his lower lip quickly.

I wanted to bite those lips and let our tongues tangle together, but I moved my eyes up to his.

"That's a very tempting offer, Emily, but that wasn't..." He paused, and I saw him visibly fight for control over his body. "That wasn't quite what I was going to offer you, my dear."

"Oh?" I gave him a look that dared him to ask me to do it.

"No, it wasn't." He pulled away, and the moment passed. His lips twitched into a smile, and he took a sip of his wine.

"Then what did you want to ask me, Dylan?" I sat back in my chair, only a little annoyed. I knew he'd make it up to me when we got back to the penthouse.

He'd been tense about something all day, but when I'd asked him, he wouldn't say what was wrong. Now here we were, in a nice restaurant, and I had to wonder what exactly he wanted to offer me.

There'd been no more talk about contracts since that one fateful night. I was glad about that. I hated those contracts. I couldn't figure what else he might want to offer me.

For a brief, fleeting moment, my heart fluttered, but then I dismissed the idea. Dylan would not be offering marriage. He definitely wasn't that kind. I had no expectations of that, although, I did sometimes fantasize about wedding dresses and ceremonies that he took part in. I didn't want to admit that to myself, not right now, and I took a deep breath to push that silly little fluttering feeling away.

"Go on, darling, what did you want to offer me?" I smiled at him and brushed a lock of hair behind my ear.

I had the blonde mop in a French twist on the back of my head, with a few strands out to soften the look. He seemed to like it, and his eyes followed my fingers.

"I wanted to... Well, I know it's probably the last thing you want to do, but you did get a degree in it, so maybe you do. I don't know." He was nervous all over again.

Now I had an idea of what he wanted to offer, and my heart melted. "Do you want me to come work with you, Dylan?"

"I do, Emily." The words burst out of him with relief. "You're not mad?"

"Why would I be mad, Dylan? I'd love to. I'm not sure what you'd want me to do, but I'd be glad to be part of the team." I grinned, touched that he thought that much of me.

Some demon in the back of my mind repeated the word traitor over and over, but I told it to fuck right off. My family didn't even know I had a degree. None had cared enough to ask me how I spent my time and didn't know I'd obtained the degree through online courses at the state university. It was their loss.

I was a free agent and owed no loyalty to people who had disowned me, did I?

Dylan was pleased and called the waiter over to order a bottle of champagne.

"What do you want me to do exactly?" I was curious and wanted to know some of the details right away.

"Well, for now, I want your opinion on things. You know this coast better than me. You know what makes the people who come here tick, what they want, what they like. You have something nobody else from my current employee pool can offer. Insider knowledge of the market here." He paused, frowned, and then rushed to speak again. "I don't mean I want you to divulge confidential information about your family's business; I didn't mean that at all."

"Dylan, it's fine. I knew what you meant, and I wasn't offended. I've actually got a lot of information to share, you're right. None of it has to do with my family's business, but I learned a lot from my experiences there. I'll be glad to be part of your team."

Our dinner and the champagne arrived, and we talked about future plans together while we ate. I was pleased, and excitement made me grin like an idiot. I would be working with Dylan, and hopefully, I would become a valuable member of his team.

I really liked the idea of having a real job. I didn't need one, but it would be nice to have something to do every day. I'd spend my days with him at work and my nights in his bed. That sounded like complete heaven to me.

EMILY

"Merry Christmas, Emily." I stretched as Dylan whispered into my ear, a broad grin on my face.

"Dylan!" I whined out because I wanted just a few more minutes to sleep. "Let me have another half hour."

"Come now, my dear. You don't want to lay in bed while there are presents under that magnificent tree you put up! They're out there, calling for you." He paused and then in a small, dramatic voice he called out, "Emily, open us. Please, you must reveal the secrets we contain. Come to us, Emily."

"Are you trying to get me out of bed with a bad Dracula impression, Dylan? Really?" I hugged my pillow tighter and grunted. "I just need five more minutes."

"Nooooo!" Dylan groaned and pulled the covers away. "Come on, show some enthusiasm."

I knew he was trying to fill my day with a little happiness, and I couldn't do much after he took the covers away but get up. "Fine!"

It wasn't a very excited fine, and I pushed up off the bed with a slight glare in his general direction. "I'm up! Let me have a minute in the bathroom, and I'll come out. Is there coffee?"

"Indeed, there is, Em. I'll go and prepare a cup for your majesty." He bowed as he slid from the bed and left me to it. I couldn't help but forgive him for waking me up.

He'd spent the days leading up to Christmas the happiest I'd seen him. We'd started work on the resort, yet, somehow, he'd managed to add a present to the growing pile under the tree every day. I went to work with him, to lunch, and came home with him, but every single day, he walked into the apartment with something in a bag that he'd leave under the tree.

I'd never been the kind to sneak a peek at the presents. My brothers would try to lift the tape from the edges of the presents to have a quick look at what they were getting. I'd always looked at the pile of presents under the tree and thought the whole presentation represented our family well.

The boxes weren't decorated with cheap and somewhat gaudy paper, as my mother called it, that other families had. Oh no, we had white boxes with silver, gold, red, or green ribbons. The colors were never mixed up, and the ribbons were never large or ostentatious. The whole display was cold to me, clinical, and the bare minimum of cheerful. I hated it. That's why the presents I'd bought for Dylan were decorated with paper that was printed with brightly colored Santas and snowmen, holly and snowflakes, and all sorts of colors. I'd even put a rather lurid amount of ribbons on the presents.

It was an in your face extravaganza of Christmas cheer, and I couldn't help but smile as I joined Dylan in the living room. He was surrounded by a fort of boxes that had started to call my name. The pile of boxes I had from Dylan were similarly decorated, and I knew he must have spent a fortune on wrapping materials. Some of those ribbons actually looked like necklaces. He smiled up at me from the floor and patted a spot at his side.

"Sit here. I know we should probably eat first, or do something that says we know how to adult properly, but I don't want to do that. You've inspired me to find that kid in me again. For once, I want to be completely immature and break into these boxes you've brought for me. Since it's just you and me, well, we can do what we want, can't we?"

Dylan had explained to me the week before that

his adoptive parents had flown down to Puerto Rico for Christmas, which meant I had him all to myself. Later we planned to make dinner and sit in front of the television watching dated Christmas movies and cartoons.

I placed my hand on his smooth cheek and looked into his smiling gray eyes. He really was magnificent. I could see the little boy that he'd never been allowed to be in the face of the grown man and finally got my brain into gear.

"Fuck adulting, Dylan. Let's do this." I leaned over, kissed him quickly, and reached for a box with the gaudiest amount of ribbons. It was the sweater I'd bought for him, and I gave it to him now. He probably wouldn't get much of a kick out of it, but I knew he'd like it. "Here, open this one first."

"Okay, you open this one." He handed me a large, thin box that looked like a clothing box and when I felt how light it was, I knew it must be some kind of clothing too. I went to pluck the ribbon away, and found out I was wrong. It was a thin gold herringbone chain necklace. I looked up at him, my eyes round with awe.

"I had to do something awesome didn't I?" he asked with a jaunty smile and just a tiny amount of cockiness. "I can't do things completely normal, now can I?"

"Thank you." I leaned over, kissed his cheek, then opened the box.

It was filled with multicolored tissue paper, and when I didn't find anything, I looked over at him perplexed. "Was the necklace the gift?"

"No, go back through the paper; it must have got stuck to one of the pieces." His eyes conveyed a message, something I didn't quite understand.

This must be something important then.

I squished the paper around until I found a round, flat piece of plastic. I dug it out of the paper and looked down at it. It was a name tag for the resort, and on it was a title and five letters I never thought I'd see.

EMILY-Director of Marketing and Sales

"You don't have to actually wear it, but all of my staff will have one. I thought you'd like to see yours now."

"Dylan…" I was speechless. Not because he'd given me a nametag as a present, but because he was giving me a chance. I've never had a real job, not one with office hours and benefits, and things like that. I was always working when it came to my family, but that wasn't the same thing, not to me. This was a real job, one that I could be proud of. "I can't thank you enough."

"It'll be my pleasure, Emily. If there comes a time when you want to move on or do something else, you just let me know. We'll figure out what needs to be done."

"This might be the best present I've ever been given." I looked down at the thin piece of plastic and really meant what I'd said. I wasn't quite sure he realized it, but that name tag was a promise of a future far more solid than the words he'd put into the last contract we'd signed.

This nametag meant permanence, home, and a place where I was needed and appreciated. It meant I was home, at last.

"Thank you, Dylan. You've given me the world on a platter, do you know that?" I meant it too. He'd opened up my eyes and given me so much. I'd started this journey on my own, but when I met him the future had changed for me. Now he was going to give me a chance to prove myself.

We went through the rest of the presents, and I was surprised when Dylan really gushed over the sweater and scarf I'd bought him. He wasn't usually a gusher, but he really liked the handmade presents.

"You know, I've been given so many things in my life, but nobody has ever bought me anything so ... suitable." The sweater was nice, and it fit him perfectly; I knew that because he'd put it on immediately. The color made his eyes stand out and enhanced his muscular physique.

"I'm glad you like it," I said with a pleased note in my voice.

"I do. Now, let's see what else is in here." He smiled a happy smile, and we went on with the opening of boxes.

I had enough jewelry now to start my own store, dresses, lingerie and a few things that didn't make sense at first, but then I thought about them and realized what they meant. There were picture frames and a very expensive vase, as well as a few figurines of lighthouses that reminded me of our time on that little island we'd visited together.

They were the kind of things his mother would have destroyed during her rages, things he'd learned long ago to put away or not purchase at all. Another promise of a very different kind of future for both of us.

"You're a very good present giver, do you know that?" I asked him once it was all opened except one last box for Dylan.

"I tried. I'm glad you like it all. It wasn't easy to get out of the resort without you noticing." He chuckled and reached for the box.

It was a large box and very heavy. He was puzzled by it but intrigued.

The sound of the paper as it tore made me wince, but I pulled my lips in between my teeth and kept my mouth shut. This was an odd present, but I thought he'd like it.

The paper revealed a wooden box, about four feet long and two feet wide. It was thin pine wood, and on the front of the five-inch-deep box was the image of a steam train passing by a mountain scene. The images were branded into the wood and gave an added hint of quality. This was a very expensive train set that I had ordered from a specialty craftsman in Colorado.

"Wow. Emily, how did you know?" He looked at me with excitement and pleasure written all over his face.

"You've stopped to look at them when we've come anywhere near toy train sets. I thought maybe you liked them." I could feel a blush forming but didn't try to hide it. I was pleased he liked it so much and felt there was no shame in showing it.

"I love them. They're just one of those things I've never thought about getting for myself. It's beautiful." He'd pulled the lid open and looked down at the set. It wasn't just a train and some tracks, there were mountains, trees, and all of the signs that would be necessary for the completed look.

"I thought maybe you could put it in your office. When you need a break you can turn the train on and watch it do its thing. You can add to it as well, and even buy terrains to go with it, you know, little replicas of the towns and areas trains go through…" I cut my words off because I knew I was rambling.

"I think that's a great idea." He pulled me to his

side and gave me a very grateful kiss. "It's wonderful, Emily, thank you."

I was pleased that we'd both had such wonderful gifts, but my stomach chose that moment to rumble. "I think we should get breakfast started now and get dinner going while we're at it."

"I think I should take you to bed first," he whispered, his eyes already that dark gray they turned when he was about to do very naughty things to me.

"You don't want to eat first?" I breathed the question against his warm lips as our eyes remained locked together. I couldn't look away; that feral look in his eyes did things to me that meant I was going to have to wait a little longer to eat. I had other needs that had to be met first.

"Eating can wait, Emily. Unless you mean eating you?" His lips pressed into mine, and his hand settled on my hip. Something went tight deep in my abdomen, and I let him pull me into his body as his lips took mine.

The crudeness of his words made that tightness strain just a bit tighter, and I wanted to groan but spoke instead. "That's just rude, Dylan, but if you're offering?"

I leaned away from him with a smirk on my face. He wasn't the only one who could be cocky sometimes.

"Oh, you know I mean more than offer, Emily." His finger trailed down my throat and to the very top button of the white cotton pajama top I had on. His finger slid into my cleavage, and I forgot how to breathe.

His lips followed, and I felt his tongue slide into the crevice, a taunting mimic of what he intended to do. He always came through on his offers.

With a sigh he pulled away and opened the tiny pearl buttons on my top. "You know very well I never say things lightly. I always…"

Dylan paused to kiss the very top of my exposed breasts before he spoke again.

"Always follow through." His hand slid between my thighs just as he finished, and his lips closed around my left nipple.

"Dylan…" I gasped as desire flared to life when his fingers found my clit, even through my pants. Thank goodness I didn't sleep in panties. My hips followed the tight circles he stroked out over the eager bundle of nerves, and I could hear how my reaction affected him.

His breathing became ragged, and I heard a faint groan every now and then that made me eager for whatever he had planned for the moment. His lips pulled away from my nipple, and I made a noise of discontent, but he only moved to the other one and captured it in a tight suction grip.

"Dylan, fuck, you do that so well." I wasn't sure

if I meant sucking my nipples or getting me off, but he did both well. My hips moved of their own will now, and I knew it wouldn't take long. I was almost there, so close I could all but feel it. "Just a little more, baby, please."

His teeth closed lightly over the nipple, and Dylan gave me one more Christmas present as I spun off into space. He hadn't even taken my pants off yet, but I didn't care. I knew he would and that he'd make sure we were both perfectly satisfied before he would let me up so we could make breakfast.

I wasn't about to complain a bit. I held him tight to me as my body shook, and I knew that I never wanted to let him go. He was much too precious to me.

DYLAN

*E*mily gave me the best Christmas of my life, and she made New Year's explosive when we spent the holiday together at Elmo's, watching an orgy as I fucked her against a glass window. They always say whatever you're doing when the clock strikes midnight is what you'll be doing all year. If I was going to get to fuck Emily all year long because of that, I wasn't going to complain. At all.

A few days later, we were back at work, and I got a call from my doctor in Kansas. He had the results of one last test, and they were ... alright. He couldn't promise anything right now, and well, I guessed nobody could. Doctors didn't like to give too many predictions anyway, not with the public's total willingness to sue, and insurance companies breathing down their necks about avoiding malpractice lawsuits, so I knew he wasn't going to go into too much detail. This was one of those wait and see kind of things.

His call jarred me out of the happy bubble Emily had surrounded me in, and it brought some rather dark thoughts to mind. What if my illness became worse? Would I die? It was always a possibility, but we all had an expiration date; we just didn't know what that invisible stamp on our forehead said. I tried to talk myself out of the dark mood I found myself in with logic. Sometimes, emotions told logic to fuck off and die, and this was one of those times.

I was in the penthouse Emily and I claimed, and I looked out over the waves crashing on the beach. There was a winter storm rolling in, and the sea was a muddy gray color with frothy white foam that crashed against the beach like an angry, overfilled washing machine in the old cartoons. That thought made me smirk, but a bolt of lightning, far out to sea, brought me right back down.

Maybe the gods hated me, and this was my punishment. There was so much uncertainty at a point in my life when I actually felt stable for once. I wanted to make plans. I wanted to say to Emily, let's do this next year, or in a few months we should do that, but I didn't know that I could think that far ahead.

A stupid thought when I'd just invested in a

resort that had cost me millions, but the resort was different. My father would take it over if something happened to me. He would know what to do with it. Emily belonged only in my hands, though. I wanted to make her promises. I wanted to talk about our future, but I couldn't guarantee I had a future to promise her.

It ate at me, and I bumped my fist against the glass of the wall. Sometimes, I wanted to bundle Emily up, pack the car, and go hide from the world in that mountain cabin my friend had loaned me. We'd been at peace there, and we'd laughed so much. Emily had seemed to like it too. I could grow a beard, and she'd let her hair grow out. We'd become one with nature and learn to live off the land.

I hated beards, and she wouldn't make it a day without those gel nails she loved so much. Which, to be fair, I loved too. The way they dug into my back made my balls go tight with exhilaration, every single time she did it.

Not for the first time, I wondered if I wasn't being fair to Emily. She had a right to know there might come a day when I'd need special care and maybe even nurses. She needed to know that at some point.

I spun away from the window, my heart breaking at the thoughts. As a man, the idea of being so weak I'd need her to help me do the most basic things just made me want to run away from it all. I knew I couldn't run away from my physiology, but I could try, couldn't I? Logic, that old demon, told me I couldn't and that it would be pointless to try.

"Fuck!" I spat out. Fuck this disease, and fuck the day it would bring me to my knees.

I would tell Emily when the time came. I knew her well enough to know that she wouldn't abandon me, not when I needed her most, but I felt like a total dick for roping her into it. Because that was what it would be. I hadn't been upfront about my health, the same way she hadn't been upfront about who she was in the grand scheme of things.

My distrust of that name of hers eased every day she was in my life, and I knew she was going to be a valuable part of my team here. For the first time in her life, Emily would have permanence. She would have a permanent address, she would know where she was every single night when she went to sleep, and she would know where she would wake up.

That was important to her at this point. I was sure a lot of people would envy the life she had before she put her foot down, but living that life would show why it wasn't all it was cracked up to be. There was a lot of loneliness with travel, especially if you traveled without a partner.

The way her family had sent her across the globe meant she'd had little time to form real relationships. The fact that an exotic dancer was her BFF wasn't so shocking when all the acts of Emily's life came together. Both Emily and Roxie were used to seeing people come and go when they'd found each other. It was almost as if they'd found kindred spirits.

Emily wasn't as bold as Roxie, and not as big of an exhibitionist, but she had the same determination and the drive to have what she wanted. I was glad the pair had found each other. Not just because I wouldn't have met Emily if they hadn't, but because Emily brought out Roxie's softer side, and Roxie brought out Emily's adventurous side. They complimented each other.

I knew Roxie would be there for Emily, if she needed her, and one day in the future she just might. I'd seen myself how strong their bond was, and I was glad Emily had Roxie.

"Baby, what are you doing up here?" Emily called out, and I turned around. That damn elevator didn't ding like the one in the other penthouse, and she'd snuck up on me.

"Hi, baby. Just checking that the paint is dry." I opened my arms, and she walked right into them without a bit of hesitation.

I pulled her close and held her to me, absorbing her warmth and affection. I felt that warmth chase away the cold edges of darkness and let my head rest on top of hers.

"I can't believe we'll be in here so soon," she said, her arms wrapped around my waist. I loved the way she breathed against my neck. Not in a sexual way, but a happy, contented way.

"Seems impossible, doesn't it?" I asked and pulled away from her. I tugged at the hand I kept entwined in mine and pulled her through. The penthouse had a large living room, four bedrooms, a kitchen, two baths, and a small room we'd decided to put a gym in. Outside, we had a private hot tub, newly installed, and a privacy fence to keep our antics away from prying eyes.

"It does, but then, I know how fast some things can happen." She walked up to the wall, placed a finger against it, and smiled when it came back clean.

The bathroom walls were painted a dark gray to match the granite of the shower tiles, and she smiled as she turned to inspect the new installation. "They did a grand job."

"That will definitely take us both." The shower had jets strategically placed to spray the entire body on all three walls, and two shower heads overhead would rain down two separate jets at the same time, if we so chose.

"The fun we'll have in here," she said and nudged my elbow with hers. I looked down and saw a teasing grin and eyes that promised a lot of sexy times would be had in this shower.

"It's too bad the heating system hasn't been installed yet." I backed her up against the wall of the shower, accompanied by the squeak of our shoes on the new tiles. "I would fuck you right here, right now, if it wasn't so damned cold in here."

"We don't have to get completely naked." Emily's voice was low and husky; it drew my eyes to her lips, and I leaned down to kiss the wet, pink flesh.

She'd started to wear less and less makeup, and I liked the change. Her clean lips were smooth and tasty under mine. She opened her mouth, and I felt her tongue snake out. I was already hard for her, and I grinned when her hands came around to grope my ass. She pushed me into her and gasped her need.

"Emily, we can't do this here right now. We'll both freeze to death," I moaned the words against her neck, just before I gently embedded my teeth in that spot that made her sigh and her knees go weak.

"Fuck, then why did you do that?" She didn't push me away or move her head to block my access' she tilted her head to invite me in for more.

"Because I want to fuck you, but my ass might fall off from the cold."

"We could go down to the car, turn the heater on…"

We were the only ones in today, so she did have a point. We could totally fuck in the car. My balls went much tighter, and I knew my dick had won the argument my brain was trying to raise.

"Come on, baby. You have a promise to keep now."

We made it to the elevator, and I kissed her the whole way down. Just before we reached the bottom floor where my car was parked, I told her the one rule I had. "If we start this, you can't stop. I don't care who might walk into that parking garage, you keep riding my dick. Understand, pet?"

"I do, sir." She gave me a playful wink, and we rushed out of the elevator and raced to my car.

We decided on the passenger seat and got in. I pushed down my trousers, and Emily pushed her pants off, luckily only a pair of white jogging pants today, and then we were in the car. At any moment a delivery van could arrive, or a maintenance worker could walk through, and it was exciting.

The idea of getting caught had us acting like silly kids, unable to fuck in a bed because they shouldn't be having sex anyway. Her lips came down on mine the instant she straddled me in the luxurious leather seat, and she sank down on me.

We groaned as I slid into her slick heat, and I guided the frantic pace of our fucking with my hands on her ass. She was as ready for me as I was for her, and for a moment, I wondered if this was panic fucking? It was insane to do this, when I could just drive her home and fuck her in a comfortable bed. It was so fucking dirty, so reckless that I didn't care.

I slid a hand between us and found her clit after a moment. "Come for me, Emily. Come so I can follow you, baby."

She could almost come on command now, but this time, it took her a moment to gather her thoughts, or maybe she just didn't want it to end. I'd have loved to have gotten her tits out and buried my face between them, but right now, it was about getting off. She thrust her hips in time with the clenching of my hands, riding my dick hard and fast.

Later, I decided. I'd take her into the playroom and make her come until she begged me to make it stop. For now, I needed to empty my balls into that sweet, succulent pussy of hers, and when her walls clenched around me, I did just that.

"Emily..." I didn't know I said her name over and over again. I just knew that I'd found sweet relief from the pressure that felt as if my balls would explode, and for a moment, pleasure beyond belief.

We breathed hard and fast, stuck together from the waist down. I needed to move, my ass was starting to get a cramp, and she made a noise of disapproval. "We need to get dressed, my dear."

"I know, but I don't want to." She sighed but pushed the door open.

I handed her the pants she'd thrown in the driver's seat and pulled my pants back up and buttoned them.

"Dylan? You don't have security cameras running yet, do you?" she asked softly and looked around.

"No, Emily, not down here anyway," I said with a soft laugh.

"Thank fuck for that. You'd have to confiscate the evidence if you did."

I shut the car door, locked the car, and we went back to the elevator, hand in hand.

"That would be worth watching a time or two, I bet." I wouldn't mind a tape of that, at all.

"No you don't, buddy. Don't go getting ideas about making a sex tape with me. I'm not one of those dimwits who thinks it's a good idea. Like tattoos of your lover's name. That's a sure-fire way to guarantee an end will come. Pure nonsense." Her southern girl came out with a vengeance, and I turned to her shocked.

"I do declare!" I fluttered my eyelashes and held my hand to my throat. "I didn't know you were such a prude, Miss Thompson."

"I'm not, you goon! I'm just sensible. Now get

me back to my office. I have a heater in there I just remembered."

"You mean there's heat in one of the rooms of this fucking cold place?" I asked, surprised. "You forgot it earlier?"

I had a sneaky suspicion that forgetfulness wasn't accidental, and the cheeky grin she gave me proved just that. The little minx.

15

EMILY

I tried to sleep that night, even though I was exhausted, I couldn't. I thought my confusion was the problem, I couldn't make my mind shut up. Doubts prickled at me and hurt stung my heart. Dylan had taken me to the playroom. That wasn't a bad thing, but it was emotionally and physically exhausting.

I remembered every moment of our time in that room. The excitement of how high he could make me go, how long he could draw out the pleasure before he'd let me reach orgasm, and finally, he made each moment in that room unforgettable. Then, fuck, the way he'd make me come until I was screaming for him to make it stop. It was incredible, magnificent, but I knew now it was a sign that Dylan was troubled. That was what hurt; there was something troubling him, and he wouldn't talk about it with me.

He had been keeping it from me for a while. The energy he expended in that room tonight wasn't the first sign he'd given me that something was on his mind, something he wasn't sharing. He'd kept me in there for a long time, drawing out the pleasure he'd given me, and the need for the culmination of that pleasure meant he'd been trying to work through something.

It really bothered me that he wouldn't talk to me. Communication wasn't a problem, normally. We talked about everything, and often, but there was something that he didn't want to talk about. Logic told me that it was something he had to work through on his own, that he needed time to get through it and make sense of it, but this had been going on for a while. He'd had time to do just that, and yet, here we were.

He was asleep beside me, but I couldn't seem to get there myself. I rolled over, pushed the duvet off my legs, and tried to find a comfortable spot, but my brain popped up with something to disturb me.

Maybe he doesn't trust you.

The only thing that would cause that would be the fact that I hadn't been forthright about my family. I argued with my traitorous brain and reminded myself that we'd got past that. He knew why I hadn't told him when we first met, and he understood why I'd kept it to myself after.

Then what could it be, I wondered. Dylan wasn't the kind to share his worries with just anyone, but he often shared concerns with me. It wasn't something he had a problem doing normally. I knew him well enough to not be worried about affairs. The man wanted me too much and spent too much time inside me for someone having an affair. I didn't think it was that, or the hotel, or even his past or his adoptive parents.

I went through long lists in my mind, trying to figure out what it was. He was healthy, or appeared to be, and he wasn't upset. He was just ... troubled. I wondered if it was money worries. People could often hide money problems, especially those who had inherited a lot of wealth. Dylan hadn't exactly inherited his wealth, yet, but he was in charge of that inheritance.

Maybe he'd squandered it on the new resort? That didn't make any sense either, I decided. He had a lot of resorts spread throughout the country. They weren't having problems, and he wasn't the kind to blow a lot of money on a pipe dream. I knew he'd considered possibilities, planned, added the numbers, and done his research before he bought the new place. That couldn't be the problem either.

Something in his past then? Maybe something he'd done...

I went still for a moment, and then I got up out of the bed. I needed something hot and comforting to drink. I must be insane to wonder if he'd committed some crime, something that had come back to haunt him.

As I waited for the electric kettle to boil so I could make hot chocolate, I revisited the thought. He could have done ... *something*. What?

He wasn't cruel, not like that. He was a dom, he loved that role, and enjoyed giving pain ... but that was in the pursuit of pleasure, ultimately, for the sub and the dom both. I couldn't imagine he'd ever take it too far. He was too controlled, too observant to ever go further than he should and hurt someone.

I went to the living room and sat on the couch with my hot chocolate a few minutes later. Nothing I thought of made sense. For a second, I thought about trying to go through his emails or phone messages, but that was an invasion of privacy too far. I'd rather just point blank ask him what was wrong before doing that.

I didn't want to force him into revealing things to me, though. Dylan would tell me, eventually. I just had to be patient. I set the cup on the coffee table and pulled a white fleece blanket over myself. It was silly to let this bother me so much.

My head had started to hurt, and the distraction was enough to make me close my eyes. The slightest bit of light made the pain worse, and the television had a red light at the base that seemed to pierce even my eyelids. There was a blue light on another device, green on yet another. So many lights.

I turned over on the couch to block the lights from my eyes. I'd go back to bed, but I had a feeling I'd be tossing around for a while longer. I didn't want to wake Dylan up, so I stayed there on the couch. It was one of the thousands of ways I showed that I loved the man, because I knew I did now.

Which was why this secret was bothering me so much. I'd realized just how much I loved him at Christmas. I felt silly, stodgy, always logical, always alone Emily was in love with the man that had made her his sub. It sounded stupid when I thought about it like that, but it was true.

It wasn't pity over his past, either; although that did make me ache for him when I thought about him as a child. Such a terrible beginning he'd had, but he'd overcome it, and his strength was one of the things that I loved.

It wasn't something I planned on revealing, not to him or anyone. I just carried it around with me. My love was my treasured little secret. He'd hinted at a future together, and we were about to move in together. He was even letting me make decisions about the new place. That did not equal love or something more.

I knew that, but at the same time, I knew this was all new for Dylan. The man obviously felt something for me, or else I wouldn't be here now. I was something new for him, something he wanted to hold on to. It could be simple infatuation, or it could be love, but I doubted he'd ever risk his heart enough to tell me.

His birth mother had destroyed his capacity to trust implicitly, but I thought I had about as much as he could give one person. I knew for a fact that I was the only woman he'd ever allowed to live with him. He was adopted by the James couple, he'd had no choice about whether he lived with a woman then, but when he'd become an adult, he hadn't allowed it. He hadn't allowed himself that human connection until I came along.

Maybe, in time, he'd allow himself to feel the things we were all supposed to feel, that we were *allowed* to feel, but for now, Dylan remained closed off.

This whole situation now was because he wouldn't allow himself to connect with me in that way. I didn't know if he saw it as a weakness, the need to connect, or if it just hadn't occurred to him that I would accept him, whatever the problems that came along.

My head started to throb the more I thought about it. I turned my head long enough to read the time on the clock on the wall. It was three am, and I was supposed to get up at seven with Dylan.

I fell asleep for a little while, but my stomach was so upset it had woken me up. I moaned a little, and tried to sit up. What was wrong with me?

I stumbled off of the couch and made my way to the bathroom. We had some pain relievers in there, and I took two with a sip of water from the sink. I decided a hot shower might help the pain in my head and crawled in. The part that should have told me that this was more than just a normal headache was the fact that I did all of this with the lights off. It hurt too much to turn the lights on.

I stood there, unmoving, while the water poured down over my head. The pain didn't decrease, but it did become more bearable. I stood there for ages, until the water started to go cold, and then I got out. After I wrapped my hair and body in towels, I made my way back to the couch and pulled the blanket over me.

My stomach rebelled the minute I put my head down, and I sat right back up. That helped the nausea, so I crammed myself into the end of the couch, and soon I'd fallen asleep again. Though it must not have been for long, my hair was still wet. The towel had come loose from my hair, and I used that as an extra pillow, too miserable to even call out to Dylan.

I doubted I'd be going anywhere when he got up, except back to bed. The nausea became unbearable. I tried to drink some more water, and that made my stomach completely rebel. I was violently sick and probably made some rather pitiful noises, but I couldn't help it.

The violent actions of my muscles only made my head hurt worse, and I began to cry because I was in so much pain. What the hell was wrong with me?

I wanted to call out for Dylan, to tell him something was wrong, but it hurt too much. The nausea seemed to finally pass, at least the vomiting did, and I moved to the tile wall. I slid down to the floor and used a towel as a cushion, but the cool wall against my temple felt good.

I fell asleep again, this time for a much longer period. My hair was dry when I woke up, the nausea was back with a vengeance. I thought it was impossible to be so sick. I hadn't eaten enough that day to throw up so very much. This time, I knew I made a lot of noise. I was exhausted, in pain, and unable to control myself. I just wanted to sleep and forget what was happening, but I was too sick.

It felt as if the vomiting went on for hours, and the sound of the flush when I felt like I was done made the pain in my head scream a whole lot louder.

I curled up in a ball on one of the rugs. My towel had come undone, and I didn't care if I was naked and on the bathroom floor. I managed to find enough energy to pull the towel over me as a blanket, even if it was still damp, and fell asleep.

This happened two more times, the pain in my head increased with each new wave of nausea, and I wondered if I was going to die, alone on the bathroom floor. What a way to die, I thought as I curled up under a blanket, reeking of vomit, naked.

I could just hear my family and peers now. She wasn't very good at being a Thompson, my father would say. I taught her to have more dignity than that, my mother would sniff. My brothers would probably sneer and walk away, if they bothered to pay attention to the news at all. My nieces and nephews might miss me, but my family, the people I'd associated with before my little rebellion?

I knew they were all wrong; this wasn't how I deserved to die. I was a strong, independent woman. I was too stubborn for my own good, most of the time, and certain of my own abilities. I was through and through a Thompson.

Right now, I was just a pitiful young woman curled up on the floor, certain she was about to die. I reached out an arm; I wanted water, I wanted pain relief. I wanted Dylan. Even the act of trying to speak hurt, used up energy, and I was too exhausted to fight off the pain.

I didn't want Dylan to find me like this, and that only made me cry harder. Something was wrong, and I was too far gone to call out to him for help.

DYLAN

*E*mily was already out of bed when I woke up and stretched out to pull her to me. It amazed me how quickly I'd come to hate waking up alone, even if it meant Emily was up already and not far away. I liked to pull her to me while we were both soft and warm from sleep, and maybe kiss her neck while my hands went down to places that were eager to be brought back to life.

Not this morning. I sighed, got out of bed, and stretched again. It was a beautiful morning, and the sun was a bright gold light that spread across the bedroom in a warm haze. Something wasn't right, I realized when I saw the door was open. I couldn't smell coffee, and Emily always made coffee when she first got up. It was the very first thing she did.

I frowned and went into the kitchen. She wasn't there, and she wasn't in the living room either.

Trudging back to the bathroom, I found the door closed, so I knocked. "Emily?"

The door opened a crack, and there was no answer, so I decided to go in and get my business out of the way. I'd barely had time to try to figure out where she was when I saw her on the floor.

I stopped and stared down at her on the floor. "Emily?"

For a second, images of the past flashed in my head, my mom as she overdosed, or the thousand times I'd woken up to go to school to find her asleep in the kitchen or the bathroom, always on the floor. That was when her dosage needed to be increased. Now, here was Emily. Emily wasn't my mother, and she wasn't on medications that would make her wander in the night.

"Emily!" I cried out, suddenly full of fear. I bent down and found her warm, to my relief, and she made a sound as I pushed to her back. "Emily, wake up, what's wrong with you?"

It all came out as one sentence, and my hands raced over her body, looking for any sign of injury.

"Dylan…" I heard her whisper. "Hospital, please. I'm so sick."

"Baby, what's wrong?" I pushed her hair out of her face and looked at her. I couldn't see that anything was wrong, and she didn't have a fever, so it must have been something internal. "Where does it hurt, what's wrong?"

"My head..." Her hand fluttered up to her head and then down to her stomach. "I'm so sick, Dylan, please."

"Alright, sweetheart, let me get you up off the floor." I picked her up in my arms to carry her into the bedroom. "Let me just run to the bathroom and get us dressed."

I knew she'd die of embarrassment if I took her to the hospital with only a towel on, plus it was far too cold, and would probably get us pulled over if a cop saw her. Fuck, why was I thinking about such stupid shit? I raced to her closet, found a long black dress that she sometimes wore out when she did errands, simple, loose, and easy to get on. I put some socks on her feet and a pair of sneakers, then threw on a pair of trousers, a black sweater, and shoved my feet into a pair of loafers.

I picked up my keys, wallet, and then her. She'd barely responded to any of it and moaned through most of the process of dressing. Whatever was wrong with her, it wasn't good. My brain wanted to race with possibilities, but I didn't have time for that. I just wanted to get her to the hospital.

Maybe I should have called an ambulance, I wondered as I glanced over at her in the passenger seat of the car. She was curled up against the window, her hand over her mouth, with her seatbelt on. She had her jacket over her head and whimpered every time I hit a bump. Emily was very ill.

When I got her into the hospital drop-off area, I parked the car and asked her if she could walk in or if she wanted me to carry her. From the depths of her jacket I heard a pitiful voice. "I don't think I can stand, Dylan. My head hurts so bad."

"That's alright, Emily. I'll get you in there, honey. Don't you worry about that." I managed to get her out of the car and carried her into the emergency department.

A woman with a bored face and very long acrylic nails looked up at me. I saw a slight roll of her eyes as she turned away from the woman beside her, and she looked at me with a look I can only describe as ... doubtful. "Can I help you, sir?"

"My girlfriend is ill, she needs to see a doctor," I stated the words as calmly as I could, despite her apparent disinterest. I knew hospital workers were overworked and underpaid, and I knew they saw a lot in their daily lives, but a little compassion for people wouldn't be unwarranted. I felt like a naughty child who had interrupted the teacher as she instructed the class.

"Well, we need her to fill out some forms, register, and then she can see the doctor."

"I don't think she can, her head hurts so bad she can't stand the light."

"If she can't fill out the forms, sir, we can't see

her." Her expression was dull, as if my problem was no concern of hers.

"Give them to me, I'll fill them out." I took the clipboard.

I let it fall to the floor and sat Emily on a chair. I'd snagged her bag too, and though I felt like I was invading her privacy, I dug around in her purse until I found her driver's license and insurance card. Emily was quiet the whole time I filled the forms out and leaned against me until I got up to take the papers to the hateful cow who had given them to me.

"She'll need to stop hiding under that coat when the nurse calls her back, sir."

I blinked at the woman, so angry I wanted to strangle her, but I didn't say anything. I swear I heard her say "druggies" as I turned away. I turned right back around.

"Pardon?" I asked, my eyebrows somewhere around my hairline.

"Nothing, sir. You can sit down now."

I stared at her and wondered why the staff in hospitals always acted like they were doing you a favor that you weren't going to pay out your nose for, all while treating you as if you were a scum of the earth. I hated the whole atmosphere and the attitudes that made you feel powerless from the moment you stepped into the place.

I let it go because Emily needed help, and quickly.

Luckily, it was quiet at that time in the morning, and a nurse came out to get Emily for triage. Emily kept the jacket over her head, but she found the strength to walk into the private office. I went with her and explained how I'd found her this morning as the nurse took Emily's vitals. Emily perked up enough to explain how she'd gone to the couch because she couldn't sleep, had made some hot chocolate, and then the nausea had hit.

The nurse asked Emily a slew of health questions, some I knew the answers to, some I didn't. Emily answered what I couldn't and denied ever having a migraine before, or being on medication for it. When the nurse asked that, a lot started to make sense.

By the time Emily was in a room and a doctor had come in, she'd started to fall to sleep. The doctor was a cheerful woman who soon had nurses and staff running around and doing their jobs. A few hours later, the same doctor, a plump redhead with a happy demeanor came in to give us news that we thought was good.

"Emily, you're having a migraine, I do believe. The hot chocolate made it even worse, I'm afraid. We'll give you a few shots that will help the pain, relieve the nausea, and I'll send you home with a few prescriptions. If the pain gets worse, you need to come in to see us; otherwise, you need to set up an appointment with your general practitioner and have this evaluated, alright?"

"Yes, thank you, doctor." Emily had her head beneath the hospital sheet still, but she was well enough to answer the doctor so that was good.

I felt relieved. Migraines were a common enough thing, but we'd have to find out why she was having them. I smiled at that thought. We would have to find out. She wouldn't go through this alone. I was already thinking of us as a team. Not long ago I'd have cringed at the idea of a 'we', but it didn't bother me at all. In fact, I felt happy about it.

A nurse soon came in and administered three drugs to Emily. She explained to Emily what the medicines were, and that Emily needed to spend the rest of the day in bed, asleep if she could manage it.

"I'll take care of her, don't you worry," I assured the nurse.

We had to wait for the nurses to be sure Emily wouldn't have an adverse reaction to the medicines, and then she was finally released. She was well enough to walk out without her jacket over her head this time. As we left, I saw the woman who had initially greeted us, and I made note of her name. I'd have a word or two with someone about her and her attitude later today.

I helped Emily get into the car then took her home. She was still quiet, but I knew that was exhaustion. She'd already said the pain was gone now.

When I helped her into bed, she hugged my neck and thanked me.

"There's no need to thank me, Emily. You needed help, and I'm glad I could give it."

"That was the worst pain I've ever experienced in my life. The nausea. Fuck, I hope I never have another one."

"From what I read on my phone while we waited, you may never have another one, ever again. We'll keep our fingers crossed, shall we?"

"Thank you."

"I'm going to pick up your medicines, get a few things at the store, and then I'll be back, alright? You get some sleep while I'm gone, and I'll be back before you know it."

I heard her mumble a reply, and she was asleep before I even left the room. Sleep was the best cure, so I left the house quietly. I thought I might have trouble getting her medicines, but the pharmacist knew me by now and only asked me to sign for her pills after I showed my ID. I didn't complain and went on to the grocery store. I bought a few things: some kind of gourmet chicken soup in a tub, some crackers, ginger ale, and a few other things she might want once she woke up.

I didn't know what else to do for her, other than provide the things she might ask for when she woke up. She was still asleep when I made it back to the penthouse, so I put the groceries away, and headed to the home office I'd set up. I needed to make a few phone calls and get that out of the way.

Emily was still asleep at dinnertime, so I made myself a sandwich and waited for her to wake up. I'd never seen a human being in that much pain. Some people might scoff, oh she had a migraine, so scary, but they haven't seen the way it hit her. She'd said she'd vomited several times, the poor thing. She'd fall asleep, wake up, throw up, then go back to sleep.

I'd had headaches that made my stomach turn, but not that bad. It must have been excruciating. And when she wouldn't let the light near her eyes, I knew how bad it really hurt. I wanted to wake her up to take the medicine, but thought that might do more harm than good. If she was asleep, she didn't need the medicine.

I didn't have a lot that I wanted to do, so I went into the living room to surf around Netflix. I found a series that looked interesting and did something I've never done before. I binged out on that series like a boy who'd just discovered masturbation and had a week to spend alone.

I didn't think I'd ever spent that much time doing nothing, and by the time Emily woke up at ten pm, I was sure I needed to find more free time. I chuckled as I got up and went to check on her. I'd paused the series several times to go check on her, and every time an episode ended I'd gone in. Now, I went in and found her awake but in darkness.

"Dylan?" she asked as I came in. "Why is it dark?"

"Because you've slept all day, sweetheart."

"You're kidding?" She slid up in the bed. "It's actually ten pm? I thought the clock was wrong and the world had ended."

"No, babe." I chuckled softly and sat beside her. "Do you want something to drink or eat? I brought you some chicken soup and ginger ale."

I brushed hair out of her face and leaned down to kiss her smiling face.

"That sounds heavenly. A nice cold drink."

"How's your head?" I saw her face was clear of pain and her eyes were alert.

"It's good, much better than it was."

"Good. I still think you should take some of the medicine, and I think you should call your doctor tomorrow."

"I'm going to, don't worry. I don't ever want one of those again."

"Good. Let me get you a drink, then I'll put the soup on."

She took the medicine and ate the soup when I brought it in, and within an hour she was asleep again. Around three in the morning I heard her cry out in agony and went in to find her rolling around on the bed. Oh dear.

"Make it stop, Dylan. Oh fuck, please, make it stop." She reached for me, and I took her hand. Yep, she was definitely going to the doctor.

17

DYLAN

Two weeks and five more migraine episodes later, and Emily had a prescription for a medicine that was meant to keep her from having another migraine. The pill was called Topamax, and her doctor put her on it because it was a trusted remedy and one of the first that would be used by any doctor. She took it, and before long, she was almost back to normal.

She had cut out caffeine from her diet, and a few other things, and she kind of walked around carefully for a bit, as if afraid the pain would attack her at any moment, but otherwise, she was doing well on it. She hadn't had a migraine since she started the medication, and that was all we'd wanted.

I started to feel relieved and started to relax a

bit myself. I'd been so worried about her that I hadn't been able to focus at work, and knowing she was reacting to the medicine well helped me to get back on track. She had even started back to work. We were days away from moving into the new penthouse, and we were both excited about it.

The only problem was, my hands had started to shake again. Not much, and not often, but I noticed it, and it worried me. I knew it was probably just stress from worrying about Emily, so I hadn't called the doctor. If it continued now that she'd got some relief and hadn't had another migraine, I'd call him, soon.

"I'm going to miss you today." She'd come into the kitchen and walked right into my arms for a hug. "I need to get my nails done, though. They're starting to look gross."

"It won't be long, and you're going to see Roxie, right?" I brushed hair behind her ear and pulled her a little tighter to my hips.

We had been perfect little angels since her first migraine, and we were starting to get tired of celibacy. The way she pushed into me and let her eyes close told me she was more than ready for some adult attention. I grinned at her as she moved her face close to mine.

"I am going to see Roxie, and maybe do some shopping, but I can't wait to get you alone later. I had the dirtiest dream about you last night and, well, I'd like to tell you about it later."

"Mm, that sounds like a story I'd like to hear." I kissed her soft lips and waited for her to open. Her tongue came out to tangle with mine, and I felt blood surge straight to my dick. It throbbed between us, and I wondered how long it would take me to come if I bent her over the counter by the stove and fucked her right here in the kitchen.

"Oh my, somebody's eager to hear that story," she whispered and moved her hand down to cup me through my trousers.

"Emily, don't start something we don't have time to finish," I begged with a groan, but she got this evil grin on her face and moved closer to my ear.

"I could just suck you off if you don't want to waste time pulling my pants down and fucking me on the kitchen floor."

"Fucking hell, Emily, don't make it worse." I didn't bother to try to hide the torment in my voice. The thought of her lips wrapped around me had my dick eager and ready to play. That merged with the image of her round ass in the air as I drove into her, and I was almost afraid I'd come in my pants if she didn't stop.

"Maybe you can jerk off in the car on the way to work." Her voice, low and husky, didn't help, and neither did that teasing look in her beautiful eyes.

"I hate you, do you know." This time there was a note of petulance in my voice, and I turned around to walk to the kitchen entrance. "You're very cruel. You know I have a meeting I can't be late for."

"I learned from the best, Dylan." Her eyes issued a challenge I would be glad to accept later. Her breasts pushed out from her chest as she leaned back against the counter, and that took all of my attention. "Later then, baby."

"Definitely later, Emily." I walked into the kitchen, kissed her cheek, and tried not to waddle out of the kitchen. I was still hard for her.

We both knew I didn't mean it when I said I hated her. If anything, I think I might be in love with the woman. I still wasn't quite ready to really admit it, but I couldn't deny that I cared deeply about her. The last couple of weeks proved that to me, without a doubt. She had become something I couldn't live without, didn't want to live without, and if I had to take care of her for the rest of my life, I'd crawl to do it.

I was stopped at a stoplight when a new thought occurred to me. My real father had been exactly the same with my mother. He'd actually given his life for her, to her. In more ways than one. He'd devoted his life to her and had never been angry at her for getting pregnant with me. I couldn't remember a lot about his life story, he'd rarely spoken about it, but I knew he'd been devoted to

Mom the moment he'd met her.

When she'd killed him, she'd killed the one person on earth who loved her above everything else. He'd loved me, of course, but Mom had been his everything. He'd taken care of her until the day he died.

I hadn't understood that kind of devotion until Emily came along. Part of me had blamed him for his own death. He couldn't change how he'd felt about her, at all. I understood that now. He'd love her completely, and despite the danger she'd put us all in, he'd tried to give her the best life he could.

If I hadn't wanted Emily to be seen by the doctor at the hospital that day, I'd have torn that woman who'd treated me with so much disgust a new one. She'd have been in a puddle of tears, and I'd have left her with a smile on my face. I'd wanted Emily to see a doctor as quickly as possible. If that meant I had to hold my tongue until it bled, that was what I would have done.

I'd never thought that kind of devotion was something I'd ever feel. I'd thought I was stronger, more hardened than my very weak father. Emily had shown me how weak I was. For her. To her, with her? I wasn't sure, but as the light changed, I knew there was little I could do about it.

I felt a tremor in my arm as I pulled into the parking garage of the new resort and tried not to roll my eyes. I was exasperated with my body, I wanted it back to normal, and the doctor had said the new medicine should do it, but I could clearly see that wasn't the case.

I felt like a complete asshole now. I sat in the now parked car and stared out at nothing. Emily had her own problems to deal with. Her family, her health, and a future of tests to be done if the migraines continued. Saddling her with me, and the future that I might have myself, was just wrong.

I couldn't walk away from her, though, and again, I imagined that was how my father had felt. For the first time in my life, I truly understood a lot of things I hadn't been able to comprehend about my father. I'd seen him as a very weak man, a pushover, but he hadn't been. He'd been a caretaker and a husband.

I didn't mind that role, now that I understood what it meant to care about a woman as much as I did about Emily. I had never even questioned why I should offer her care. I could have told her to go back to her own place and deal with her problems, but it hadn't occurred to me to do that. There had simply been no question that I would make sure she recovered.

Something told me she felt the same way. That she'd do the same for me, which was the big difference between my parents and us. Emily wasn't broken. Not like my mother had been. She would have to make sure she took care of herself, but she was the kind of woman who would manage if it came down to it. She would take care of me if the time came, and she wouldn't begrudge me a moment of her time. It would just be another chapter of our relationship to her.

I was sure there were people out there who would say I should have let her go a long time ago. It wasn't fair to not tell her that I might become very ill one day. I just couldn't admit it to her right now. Yet again, I thought about how it was dishonest to keep it to myself.

My eyes caught my reflection in the windshield, and I stared at myself. You couldn't see that there was something wrong with me, that there were things happening in my brain and nerves that might mean I'd become unable to walk, or breathe, at some point. There were no outward signs that I was a ticking time-bomb.

I wanted to paint the word liar over that reflection, but it wasn't really a lie, was it? It was withholding information, but not a lie. I knew I'd have to tell her at some point, but for now, I was keeping it to myself.

The sound of a car coming into the parking garage snapped me out of my reverie, and I got out of the car. I had a meeting with the designer, and had to hand over some of the plans that Emily had suggested. Work had begun, and there were workers all over the place now, repairing, building, and preparing the dream I could already see coming true.

I went up to my office, the first full room to be prepared, and made sure my personal assistant was ready for the day. He was ready for me and had the coffee on already when I got in.

"Hi, Dylan. Your appointment isn't here yet, so if you want to get settled in, I'll buzz you when she arrives." The tall, dark-haired man with light blue eyes handed me a cup of coffee.

"Thanks, Rick. Can you order a dozen roses for me, please? Pink and white. Have them brought here this afternoon, and I'll fill in the card before I go home."

"Can do, Mr. James."

I closed the door to my office and went to my desk. I knew I didn't have long, but I checked my emails and answered a few before Rick buzzed me.

The rest of the morning was quiet after the meeting, and I ordered lunch. Emily would come in this afternoon and we'd get a few more things done before heading back to the penthouse. It wouldn't be long before heading home meant riding the elevator up to the penthouse here.

My adoptive parents were happy for me that I'd found someone I wanted to share my life with, but I knew they'd rather have me based out in Kansas. I would have to move some of my people from out there out here, if they made that decision, and the base of operations would change to here. That also meant longer flights when I had to go out to the west coast properties, but I'd deal with it.

I wanted to build something like a normal life here with Emily, and I wanted to start to delegate some of my responsibilities to others. That would mean less traveling and more telecommunicating, but it was something I'd have to do. Especially if my illness progressed. My parents didn't know about that part, I hadn't told anyone, but I knew that when I did tell them that they'd understand my reasoning.

Emily came in right after lunch with sparkling nails and a happy face. "We had the biggest hamburgers for lunch!"

"Ah, good, you've eaten." I pulled her into a hug and wondered how soundproof my walls were. The red of her nails was giving me ideas about how it would feel to have those talons scratching down my back.

"I have. I'm going to head up to the penthouse and have a look, want to join me?"

"Yep. I haven't been up there yet. Let's go have a look."

"Want to stop the elevator?" She'd been quiet while we waited for the elevator, but as soon as the doors closed behind us, she got chatty.

"I would rather ride the elevator up and fuck you on our new bed." I moved in front of her and put my hands on the wall on each side of her head. "I love fucking you in elevators, but I'd rather take my time."

I looked down to see her teeth catch her lip in a soft bite of anticipation. "You promise?"

"You know I don't say things I don't mean, Emily." I inhaled the scent of her perfume and wished I hadn't told her we'd wait. I kind of liked the idea of her on her knees sucking me off, but it had been a while for both of us. I wanted to make sure she was satisfied too.

"I know you don't." Her hands came up to clutch at my chest, and her eyes glanced at my lips before she looked up into my eyes. "Can't this thing go any faster?"

"Almost there, baby." Just to increase her anticipation, I let my hand slide into the waist of her pants and down into her panties. "Doesn't mean I can't get things started, though."

She gasped and then moaned as I slid a finger inside of her. She was already soaking wet and ready for me. I knew she loved sex as much as I did, so I wasn't the least bit surprised. "You're so ready for me, Emily."

"I left Roxie before we even managed to get any shopping done. I just wanted to get back here to you." Her eyes closed as she spoke, and I stroked into her deeper, enough so that my palm was pressed into that most sensitive part of her.

"Then let me give you what you need, Emily." The elevator stopped, and the doors opened. Time to play.

EMILY

Thank fuck the migraines went away. That's all I could think about that. I've never felt that terrible in my life and didn't want to feel it again. The medicine the doctor gave me helped, but when they kept coming back, despite the pain medicine, he'd put me on a medicine that was supposed to prevent them, and I'd kiss him the next time I saw him.

I wasn't about to take being pain free for granted ever again, not after that. Especially when Dylan was a part of my life now. He was so handsome and sexy, that not having sex with him actually started to depress me. I'd be in between migraines, looking at him and wanting him, but too tired to do anything about it.

Now, my energy was back, and so was my desire for him. He'd rocked my world in our new penthouse earlier, but I needed more. After dinner, I went into the office where he was typing up an email to his adoptive father and made him an offer he couldn't turn down.

"If you want to have me again, Dylan," I paused to make sure he looked up to see me in the black lace nightgown and black heels, "you're going to have to catch me. And maybe tie me up."

I held up the rope I'd found in his play room and when he went to stand up, I ran away. Only, I cheated, because I ran straight into the bedroom. When he caught me, he lifted me into the air, and I wrapped my legs around his waist.

"You want to play, pet?" His eyes were as hungry for me as mine were for him.

"You know I do." My lips found his, but that didn't stop him from walking me to the bed. He dropped me and studied the length of rope I'd had in my hand.

"I think we can make use of this."

I stretched out on the bed and waited for him to tie me up. I thought he'd just tied my wrists to the hooks on the back of the headboard, but he went a little further.

Each wrist was tied off to one side of the headboard, and then he took my feet in his hands. I wanted to ask him what he was doing; if he tied my feet together, I couldn't open my legs, but then it all became clear.

With a rather wicked laugh he pushed my legs back, until they were over my head. Dylan has tied me up dozens of times now, and I've found it's something I like, especially when it's outside of his playroom. He's more playful, less dominant, but still a sensual beast when he ties me up outside of that playroom.

When he had my legs tied to the headboard, I had a better idea of what he had planned. He was positioned in front of me with my pussy on full display. It was like he'd created a table of delights for himself, and all he had to do was lean his head down to partake in the offerings.

"Yes, I like this. Is this what it was like in your dream, Emily?"

I'd told him about my dream at the other penthouse. I just hadn't realized he'd want to turn it into reality so quickly. I wasn't about to complain.

"Very much so, sir." I grasped at the ropes that connected me to the headboard and shifted around a little. "I knew you'd like it."

"I do indeed." His eyes were on my most intimate parts, bare and ready for his touch. Delight shot through me, mixed with a strong hint of pleasure, and I bit the inside of my lip to stop myself from begging him to touch me already.

Normally, when we weren't in the playroom, Dylan didn't bring out the toys, though he would sometimes. As I rested there, tied expertly to the bed, I wanted to ask him to get the nipple clamps. They heightened my awareness and made my nipples tingle with electrifying pleasure. I wanted that a little bit more.

"What else do you want, pet? I can see it on your face, something is missing." His fingers reached out to touch me, but I was disappointed when he only trailed his fingers down my ass.

"It's okay. I just want you to touch me." I shivered as his smooth hand slid up my thigh, along my calf, and back down to run over my ass. "More, Dylan."

"Not until you tell me what it was you wanted, pet." His hand moved closer to the place I wanted him to touch me the most, and I let my head fall back.

His teasing would kill me. He'd keep it up, until I broke and told him, so I might as well get it over with.

"I want the clamps."

"The suction cups or the metal clamps that squeeze your nipples so tight it aches when I let them go?" His hand went up my leg without missing a beat before it came right back down.

"The suction ones. Just those." His fingers slid a little closer this time, and then, on the next run up my leg, I felt him touch me softly, just there, on the edge of the most womanly part of me. Then his fingers slid away to explore up my leg again.

"Alright. I won't be a moment." He left me, and I sighed, my head propped on the pillows.

He was right, we might as well do this right if we were going to do it. No need for half measures here.

He was back in seconds and leaned over me to attach each of the small suction cups to my nipples. His tongue licked the first nipple, and I felt it all the way down to my clit. His fingers pinched the tight bud and applied the cup before he did the same to the other. I really loved the things and was glad he'd finally forced me to ask for them. I felt the blood as it tried to throb into the constricted skin, and it made my head swim with how good it felt.

I was focused on the sensations, on how it felt as if I had two mouths on my nipples and couldn't stop the way my hips tried to twist around. "Thank you, Dylan."

"You're very welcome, pet." He moved back to kneel in front of me, and his hands slid beneath me to tilt me just right. "Now, let me focus on what really matters."

His face came in close, so close, but he didn't touch me. Not yet. This was a tease I'd become familiar with, but that didn't mean my body knew it. My thighs tensed, and my back arched as my body tried to force him to touch me. He knew the game, though, and remained out of reach.

"You're so wet for me, Emily. You smell so

fucking good. I know you're going to taste just as sweet as you always do. Like my own private candy stash that nobody else gets to touch."

I was focused on his words with my ears, but my body was still caught up on the sensation from my nipples. I needed more, I needed his touch. "Dylan, please. Make me come."

"Earlier didn't take the edge off that hunger of yours then, pet?" His fingers stroked down one side of my labia, and I tensed all over again. The next stroke saw two fingers stroke me, one on each side, and my jaw clinched in anticipation.

Soon, he'd touch me, but only when he decided I was ready. Not before then.

"How are those clamps, pet? Do you want them tighter?"

"No!" I said quickly, they didn't need to be changed at all. I just needed him to touch me. Soon.

"Good. Let me know if they need to be changed."

I knew he wouldn't let me come, not until I was a whimpering mess, and he had me twisted up into knots that might never come loose. It was the kind of torture I'd craved from him from the moment I'd met him.

He knew how to give it to me just right.

"Thank you, sir."

He cupped my wet mound then, and I felt the squeeze of his fingers on me as an excruciating new tease. He wasn't touching my clit directly, but it was touched. "Mm, that's so good, sir."

"Thank you, pet. Now, don't move." His head lowered, and his hands tilted me just right to allow his tongue to delve into me.

His wide tongue flattened on me and gathered every drop of my desire that he could get. My fingers grasped at my bonds, and my body tried to move in the normal response, but my legs were over my head. "Sir…"

"Easy now, pet. It's alright." His lips closed over the skin there and sucked at me for a long moment that I thought would see my head explode.

I wanted to scream at him to let me down, to flip me over and fuck me until I couldn't take anymore. I wanted to tell him to suck my clit, but my mouth wouldn't form words; it was all too good and my brain just wouldn't function.

"Dylan…" was all I could manage as his tongue flicked at me in tight circles. "Fuck, don't stop, please don't stop."

It was a tossup with Dylan. Sometimes he'd listen to me, at other times he'd do exactly the opposite of what I'd demanded. It just depended on his mood. I had a feeling he was going to make me wait, but I guessed he took pity on me.

Instead of stopping to move to some other area to torture into raw awareness and need, he began to suck at me, and that set me off. I screamed his name, my hands straining against my bonds until I knew there'd be marks.

I didn't care, I'd wear wide bracelets for a week if I had to. All I cared about was the way my body exploded, the way something went tight, so damn tight, before it began to flutter in a pattern that sent me into orbit.

That was the moment when Dylan displayed his skills with tying knots. A tug of his finger and my feet came down from the headboard and fell to either side of his body. In an instant he was deep inside of me, and he rode me right back up that precipice I'd started to come down from.

I could barely feel my legs, but my arms wrapped around him as he held me close. His arms were buried under me as his hips pounded into me, hard and fast. I'd thought he'd drag this out, but he surprised me with how fervently he needed me. There was something almost desperate in the way he drove his body into mine, and I held onto him for dear life.

I could feel my nails digging into his back as I exploded all over again, but I couldn't stop the way my fingers clenched, or how deep I scratched him when my hands slid down his slick back. We were both covered in sweat, lost in each other, in pleasure, to notice that the new pleasure we felt was wrapped in pain.

When I lifted my head away, he nipped my chin

and then started to kiss me. He tore his lips away with a groan, and I took the moment to inhale deeply.

"You are mine, Emily."

I had said it a hundred times to him, but it was something he needed to hear. It wasn't necessarily ownership that he was proclaiming, though. It was his own emotions that he declared with that statement. He wanted me, he needed me, and he was mine as much as I was his. It was a moment that revealed just how vulnerable Dylan could be, hidden by the ownership claim.

"I am yours, Dylan," I told him, my breath a pant at his ear. "You are mine."

I clenched around him, my arms, my legs, my pussy until he suddenly came to a halt, just before his hips began to jerk into me.

"I'm coming, Emily. Fuck, I'm coming."

That's when something occurred to me. I thought I was due for my birth control shot. I went still beneath him and assured myself that everything I had read said it would take six months to get pregnant after the shot. Was that always the case?

I didn't say anything to him. I just snuggled into his side and let my thoughts wander. Surely my gynecologist's office would have called to remind me, though? Of course, they would, I reassured myself. With a sigh of relief, I got out of the bed and headed for the shower.

Dylan joined me, and we took the time to wash each other before we went to watch a movie in the living room. I'd decided to call the gynecologist tomorrow to find out when I needed to come in, and I didn't worry about it anymore.

I wasn't ready to have a baby, not yet. I wasn't sure I really wanted to have kids. I did, but at the same time, I wasn't sure it was something I should do. I wasn't in a totally committed relationship. Dylan and I had never talked about children, other than the mention of birth control when we first met.

It wasn't something I'd ever thought I'd have, not with the way my life was with my family. I wouldn't have time to find a partner, much less get pregnant. Then, when I'd rebelled, I'd been looking to live and experience life, not strap myself with babies. Maybe someday, but not right now.

We went to sleep after the movie, and I didn't worry about it anymore after that. I was too tired to worry, and the need to sleep overcame any lingering doubts. I was wrapped in Dylan's arms, safe and warm, locked away from the evils of the world. We'd dealt with my migraines, and we were about to move into a new home that we'd designed together. We'd even picked out the furniture together. We had a brand new life waiting on us, and I couldn't wait.

I snuggled closer to Dylan, even in my sleep, and found comfort from his nearness. Even unconscious, I needed the man who had made the world come alive for me.

DYLAN

I spent the morning with Emily, in the bed of our old home for the last time. We were going to our new home tonight, and I couldn't wait. I had a meeting with a candidate for the head of staff, and other than that, our day was free.

When I'd made her scream my name for the third time, I finally let up and rolled over to my side. She cradled herself next to me, and we both caught our breath. I tugged at her hair absentmindedly, the silky strands sliding through my fingers always a fascination for my unconscious mind. It was something I did often, without realizing it.

"Do you want breakfast, darling?" I asked, my brain still not totally functional.

"I think we have a Danish left. We haven't been

to the grocery store since we're leaving here tonight."

"That will work. It sounds so empty in here now, without all of our stuff." I still hadn't moved, and she didn't show any signs of wanting to get up either.

It didn't bother me. All I wanted to do was lie there until I could feel my legs again.

"It does, but we'll be in the new place tonight. Although, I will miss that pool."

"That's why we have the hot tub. Not as good for exercise, but we can find other things to do in it." I could hear how dirty my chuckle was, and that made me snort.

"Are we just two sex perverts who can't get enough of each other?" she asked with a hint of laughter.

"Nymphomaniacs, you mean. We could be. Only for each other. I don't have the energy, or the desire, to fuck anyone else."

"You wear me out too, you know? My poor legs are still shaking underneath the covers." She glanced down and laughed again.

"I know, I can feel them." She pinched my side when I said that, and I finally slid out of the bed. I ran to the kitchen, microwaved the sweet pastries in the package they came in, and brought the carton of orange juice in. "I thought there was no sense in dirtying up dishes; we'll live decadently."

"That's fine, I just need something cold to drink to take my medicine." She reached for the pill box she used to keep track of her dosages, and popped one of her pills in her mouth. "That's done then. I'll shower and head over to the new place with the last of the boxes, shall I?"

"I'll help. I don't have that meeting until lunch time."

I'd hired a cleaning agency to come in and clean the place up after we left, and I'd arranged for the keys to be delivered to the agency that rented the place out. I was kind of sad to leave it, but at the same time, glad to. I'd dismantled everything in the play room and thrown most of it away. I'd kept the toys and the restraints, but the rest of it? I didn't think I needed it anymore.

Emily satisfied me in ways that I didn't know a woman could. I wouldn't give up the dom role completely, but I didn't need the room to hide away in anymore. I hadn't told Emily yet, but she'd figure it out soon enough.

We moved the last few boxes down to her car and mine then went up for one last look around. I hadn't left anything, and neither had Emily. We were free now to go live our new life, and I couldn't wait. We even had our first meal planned already. Emily would go to the grocery store while I was at my meeting, and we'd cook the meal together later.

I carried down one last bag of trash, disposed of

it, and we headed to the new place. Emily had already unpacked most of the boxes, and the new boxes, plus some from my old office that I hadn't unpacked yet, would be sorted today.

We had new furniture in the house, and a very luxurious bed to sleep in. The kitchen appliances were all brand new and state of the art, and we'd decided to add in a lot of small appliances like mixers and cookware because we both liked to cook. It would be a dream come true for anyone who loved to cook, and to us, it was.

It was the highlight of the penthouse, for us, in fact. Recessed lighting and four long windows along one wall provided plenty of light. A long countertop added workspace that was supplemented by an island about eight feet long that would also serve as a workspace. The fridge, stove, and microwave were all on the other side of the room where the sink was located, along with more space for cooking.

The bathroom was small, with only a shower and a small tub that Emily kept calling a hip-bath. That we decorated in dark blue tiles with a good amount of light. The living room was small too, and we'd put a wraparound couch in there with several sections that folded out in recliners. A large television dominated one wall, since we both liked to watch movies, and if we didn't feel like watching movies, we had a great view of the night sky over the ocean.

Our bedroom was in the back, and there was only one window. It was on the side facing the land, and there was too much light back that way, so we'd hung blackout curtains in there, in an almond color. The bedding matched the curtains, but the plush carpet on the floor was a dark chocolate brown. There were two large closets and two chests of drawers.

The other rooms were still empty, but we'd fill those with something later. For now, we had all that we needed. We'd been so eager to start our lives here that we'd decided to go ahead and move in without filling the other two rooms.

"I'm going to get a shower, Emily. I need to get ready for that meeting."

"Alright. I'll get ready to go too." She pecked me on the lips and left the kitchen to head into the bedroom. Her clothes were already in her closet, so she didn't have to do that today, at least.

We left around the same time, and it wasn't long before I'd made it to the restaurant. It was a new place that offered cuisine from several different European locations. I'd wanted to check it out to see what was offered and to sample the dishes. We had to decide what to have in ours that would make it stand out. There was also the added benefit that when I opened, I'd be able to tell my customers the good places and the bad.

I planned to interact with our guests periodically, especially those who rented the penthouse and suites. A waiter quickly came to seat me when he found out I had a reservation, and from the looks of it, that decision had been a good one. The place was full. That was a good sign. I ordered a glass of beer and told the waiter I'd wait for my guest before I ordered.

Her name was Michelle Gilder, she was in her mid-fifties, and had lost her last job when the resort she worked at was taken over by another corporation. The new owners had decided to replace everything, including the staff, good and bad, and she'd gone with them. Her resume spoke of loyalty, hard work, and came with professional references that glowed about the woman. She had experience managing staff, and I thought she'd be a perfect fit for us.

"Hi there, Mr. James, I'm Michelle Gilder; it's nice to meet you."

I pulled my head up from the file I'd been studying and smiled as I stood. "Hi, Michelle. Please take a seat."

"Thank you." She looked around, and I could see she was pleased with the place. It wasn't very expensive, but it was also a treat to eat at a place like this.

"Here's the menu, what would you like to drink?"

"Coffee, please," she said to the waiter with a kind smile.

"Great. Let's decide on what to eat, shall we?" I wasn't nervous, but I did find these kinds of meetings sometimes impersonal.

My adoptive father had taught me that this was an important part of hiring senior staff, however. You got a chance to judge how they treated those in lower positions, and you could get a glimpse of how they would treat your employees. I didn't want someone who treated my staff like they were replaceable. I wanted to garner loyalty and prevent loss through high turnover rates.

My brain was in business mode, but the lunch went smoothly, and the woman with curly brown hair met my expectations. She treated the wait staff kindly and with a smile, she was able to answer my questions eloquently, and she had a firm understanding of what the position entailed. She'd also managed to make me laugh a few times and had put me at ease.

I liked that about her.

"I'd like to offer you the position, Michelle. I'd like you to come into the resort and make a decision. It will be another month or two before we officially open, but I'll need you before that. I need to start the hunt for staff right away and you and I will work together to hire some of the more senior staff. We can talk about salary, benefits, things like that, if you're interested. I've been looking for someone who understands my vision, and I'm pretty sure you do."

Brown eyes lit up with happiness, and she gave me the brightest smile I'd ever seen. "I'd be glad to, and yes, I think I understand your vision well. Your staff will be safe with me."

"Good. Now, how did you like your meal?" I sat back and waited for her answer.

"It was lovely, something I've never had before, but I liked it." She looked down at the empty plate and then up at me.

She didn't say anything about how long the plate had sat there, something I'd done as a test, when I asked the waiter to leave it before she came. I'd asked him to do several things, like bringing her white wine instead of what she'd order to drink, and to spill a glass of water on the table.

She'd responded nicely, but without fear of correcting the order, and she'd helped the man to clean up without complaint. She'd earned herself a gold star so far.

"I've never had chorizo served like that myself. It was nice, a very good choice. Would you like dessert?"

"No, thank you, I'm too full. It was a wonderful meal."

"Great. I'll have my assistant call you, and you two can set up a date to come in and have another talk. If you want to go now, you're free to do so. I think I'm going to stay and try the dessert." She stood, her bag under her arm, and I stood with her.

She held her hand out, and I took it to shake. "Thank you, Mr. James. I really look forward to hearing from your assistant. Thank you for giving me a chance. I know I'm an older woman, but I promise, you won't regret it."

"Shhh, I don't care about your age, just how well you can do the job. You have a great day now, Michelle. It was a pleasure to meet you."

"Thank you." She beamed at me before she left.

I felt good about my decision to hire her, if she accepted, and I had no doubt she would. I sat to speak to the waiter.

"Thank you very much for your help, Tim. There will be a nice tip in it for you." I gave him a wink, and he took the plates away.

"No problem, Mr. James. Would you like desert?" He was as attentive as ever, and for a moment, I thought about trying to poach him from the restaurant.

"No, but thank you, everything was excellent. I'll make sure to leave some flyers from the restaurant in the resort if you'll bring me some with the bill."

"Thanks, that would be great." He walked away,

happy, As I waited, I glanced down to the entrance and saw none other than Trent Thompson.

For a man who was always jet-setting around the world, he seemed to be awfully focused on Myrtle Beach lately. My blood boiled when I looked at him, and thoughts about how he'd treated Emily flooded in. That didn't help, but I had to remain calm. I paid for the meals, left a hefty tip, and slid the flyers for the restaurant into my folder.

I would avoid Trent, somehow, and just walk right out of the place.

Tim brought back my slips to sign, and I stood to leave. That was about the time Trent walked past me, and I bumped into him.

"Oh, it's you again. They'll let anybody in here, I see." Trent's upper lip curled, and something just popped in my head.

"Yeah, scum that disown their sister over nothing is pretty low." It was out before I could stop it, but I didn't back down.

"What did you say?" His jaw went hard, and he squinted at me.

"I said, letting in scum that disown their sister over nothing is pretty low. I don't know how you could have done that to someone as delightful, beautiful, talented and beyond fucking loyal as Emily is. She's the most kind, caring, compassionate person I've ever met, and you and your tired little family kicked her out because she's dating me? That's trifling, man."

"Let me tell you..." Trent started to say, but I held my hand up.

"Believe it or not, Trent, I don't give a fuck what you have to say. I've won, you lost. I have the resort I wanted, and I have the most amazing woman in my life. In fact, having her makes me the winner for life, because she's brought something to me that you obviously never understood you had. You had an angel in your midst, and you threw her away. Like I said, trifling."

I could see Trent wanted to swing at me, and I stood there, jaw ready, but he just walked away. Good for him.

20

EMILY

There were moments in your life where everything slowed, became surreal, and you just watched, like a spectator at a theater. As if what was happening was happening to someone else, not you. That was what I was experiencing now as I looked at the name on the envelope.

A week after we'd moved into the new penthouse, I'd received a letter. From my brother Trent. The last one I got nearly tore me apart, and I wondered now what kind of fuckery he was trying to perpetrate. Dylan had told me about his run-in with Trent at lunch, but we hadn't heard anything and assumed the matter was dropped. Now, I had a letter from him.

I put it down and decided I wouldn't focus on it for now. I had work to do and later, when Dylan was here, we'd open it together. Not just because I had decided there were to be no more secrets between us, but because I needed his support to open the damn thing. I took a deep breath, finished my coffee, and then rode the elevator down to meet with the designer. She was really fun to be around, and we were ahead of schedule because of the incredible work she and her team were doing.

The resort hadn't needed a ton of work to get up to standards, but painting the walls, putting in carpet, and then adding the furniture would take a while. Some of the rooms wouldn't even have furniture for another month or two after we opened, because we had so many to fill. Of course, the suites and the penthouses required more work, and we were about to start on those today.

As it turned out, right now, I just did whatever Dylan needed me to do, and today, that was helping Erica set up the penthouse closest to ours. "Hi, Erica, I'm here."

"Oh, good! I need to know what you think about these plates. Are they suitable? Dylan and I liked them when we chose them, but I'm not so sure now."

I inspected the plates, white with swirls of pastel blues, greens, and pinks running over them. They were festive and looked quite expensive. I liked them, though, more than anything, and that made up my mind. "I like them. They'll be fine."

"Good. That's settled then. Alright, let's decide where the furniture goes, shall we?"

I knew she and Dylan had drawn up plans for each penthouse, but as I'd learned already, plans were made to be broken in this business. Odd walls that stuck out in places prevented a couch from sitting back properly or curtains didn't quite measure what they should. It was a game of adaptation, and I'd learned to play it well.

Of course, my previous life had taught me that lesson too, but I refused to talk about that right now.

I walked into the bedroom, which had charcoal gray carpet, and looked around. There were two windows in here, and the plan had been drawn up to face the bed toward them. "From what Dylan and I had learned already, the glare from the neon signs everywhere and the streetlights reached even up here. I thought it would be dark up here, but it isn't. I'd put the beds against the other wall, put in blackout curtains, and situate the room like that."

Meaning exactly the same way we'd done ours. Workers moved the bedframe and began to put the bed up. We walked out into the kitchen, and I found the stove top we'd ordered didn't quite fit. There was a hair's difference, and luckily, another worker came in and shaved down the problem spot with a chisel and utility knife. By the time the stove was installed, you couldn't tell the countertop with a thin veneer of granite had been chipped away at all. "Good job."

The workers grinned and moved on to putting in the sink. Erica and I went into the bathroom and hung up shower curtains, a few wall decorations, and the towel racks/warmers. We weren't just pretty faces around here, that was for sure, and Erica was definitely one to get down in the mud and do what needed doing.

It wasn't a bad day, but I had that letter in the back of my mind, no matter how hard I tried to ignore it. I went out to lunch with Erica and still couldn't stop thinking about it. I tried to distract myself with a decadent chocolate dessert, but even that didn't help.

What did he want now?

I chewed at my nail as Erica drove us back to the resort, and I apologized for being so silent during lunch.

"It's no problem, Emily. I know there's a lot going on in this place, and a lot to worry over. I don't think you're rude at all, so don't apologize again. Let's see what else we can get done to ease that worried mind of yours."

That was Erica. She found peace through work. I started to unpack dishes and loaded them into the newly installed dishwasher. I put in the soap tablets and started the load. We wanted everything clean and sanitized when our first customers came in.

"Emily? Dylan's called, he said your phone is off?" Erica came out of the guest room and handed me the phone.

"Yes, I turned it off earlier and forgot to turn it back on. Thank you."

"Hi, Emily, what's up, darling?" I heard his voice, and my heart melted and I smiled for the first time in an hour or more.

"I'll tell you later. What's up?"

"Nothing, I just wanted to check on you. How's your head?" He must have been on his lunch then. I sat in a chair at the kitchen table. They were sturdy director's chairs in off-white linen. Maybe not overly practical, but we figured most people in the penthouses wouldn't be eating in often anyway. We'd gone for attractive over practical in this instance.

"My head is fine, actually. Really good. The paint fumes are all gone, and I can't smell anything else." I wanted to ask him to come and see me, but we were both busy, and that stupid letter could wait until we were together later. For now, I'd let it go.

"Good, I'm going to get a burger, and then I'll be back in the office if you need me."

"Enjoy your lunch, darling. See you later." I hung up the phone and took it back to Erica. "Thanks for that. I'm going to go over and check the other penthouse, see how the beds are in those and check the couches."

"Great. I'm just getting the curtains up in the guest bedroom. I'll join you in a bit."

I walked into the penthouse and checked that everything was alright. The three penthouses were basically the same layout, but each one had its own quirks. I knew I didn't have to do any of this, but I really wanted to avoid that letter. If I went back to the penthouse alone, I might open that letter.

If it was more abuse from my brother, Dylan would find me in a flood of tears. If that happened, he was liable to hunt Trent down and beat him to a pulp. Not that Dylan was the violent kind, but I saw the way the mention of Trent and how my family had treated me made his demeanor change. He went from happy, calm, and collected, to icy cold, distant, and hard all over.

I didn't want the whole thing to get worse. I'd cry if it was more of Trent's shit, but if he was there, I wouldn't feel so alone. He'd be there to reassure me and help me to throw the damn letter away.

I couldn't hope that it was good news, though, I supposed it could be. Trent, for whatever reason, had gone back to dick mode when it came to me and Dylan. I thought his wife had calmed him down, brought out a softer side to him, but I hadn't seen that side in a while now. He had probably found a way to cut me out of the family money, though I doubted even Dad would go that far.

Dad might not have been the most loving man to grow up with, but he'd loved me in his own way. I'd been his only girl, and for the longest time, the only child who stuck by him. The boys had gone off into the world to sow their oats and do the stupid things that I'd had to clean up. I'd been by my father's side, and I'd helped him with that crazy scheme of his when he decided it was time to call the boys home.

Which was part of the reason it had hurt so much when my father agreed to cut me out. I'd wondered if it was another scheme, if he was doing this to teach us all some lesson, but I hadn't heard from him. After a while, I'd started to think even he had truly disowned me.

I'd learned to block the pain out, and Dylan did his best to keep me happy. He went above and beyond quite often, and I couldn't repay him for that. He was the only reason my family's abandonment hadn't crushed me. He would get me through whatever fresh hell Trent wanted to throw at me. I just knew he would.

I managed to get through the rest of the day without breaking down in tears or running to the penthouse to tear the letter open. Part of me felt like I owed it to Dylan to open that letter with him there, and so, as much as I wanted to get it over with, fear and that decision made me put it off. I was a mess by the time I went back to the penthouse to start dinner.

I burned the spaghetti sauce I'd made, and the frozen bread dough hadn't thawed out on the counter. When the pasta burst into flames in a pot of water, I threw it in the sink, turned the stove off, and burst into tears. I was like that when Dylan came home and walked into the kitchen. I hurried and wiped at my face with a paper towel as he came in.

"Emily, what's wrong, honey?" He knelt in front of me as soon as he saw my face. A quick look at the cooking area explained some of it. "Oh no, what went wrong?"

"It's my fault, I'm too distracted. I've never cooked on an electric stove before, and it's not the same as gas stoves. I just, I don't even know how the pasta caught on fire, it was in a pot of water, for fuck's sake. I'm just, I don't know, I'm useless today!" I let my head drop down on my folded arms and couldn't help it. I started to sob again.

"It's no problem, Emily, we'll have something delivered. Don't worry about the food. Come into the living room with me. Come on, forget this stuff."

I wanted to sit at the table and put off going into the living room. The letter from Trent was in there on the coffee table, and I didn't want to go near it. I even dug my heels in as we walked into the room. The sun had started to go down, and the room was dim with only a lightbulb on. Dylan glanced at the paper on the table but didn't really look at it.

"Your phone has been off all day, and now you're here in tears. Tell me what's wrong and who I have to kill." He sat in the corner of the couch and pulled me down with him.

I stretched out on the couch and leaned my head on his chest. "I've just, I got something in the mail today."

"Alright? Who from?" I could see his jaw going tight already, and his eyes had narrowed.

I put my hand on his jaw and tried to work that knot loose that had appeared at the side of his face. It wasn't that hard to figure out, not with how I reacted the last time Trent sent me a letter.

"My brother." I closed my eyes when I heard an angry sound rumble up through his chest.

"Which brother, Emily? You have a few." He wasn't being nasty to me, just clarifying.

"Trent."

"That fucking bastard." He scrubbed at his jaw, took a deep breath, then looked down at me. His hand came up to cup my face now, and his thumb stroked at my cheek to comfort me. "What did it say? Why didn't you tell me? Oh, Emily, why did you carry this around with you all day? I could have helped you."

"I didn't. Not really. I haven't opened it yet. You've been busy, and I had things to do too. I saw it after you left and thought I'd wait until tonight to open it. When we were here together, and I wouldn't have to be such a mess. Didn't work really, though, did it?"

"No, it doesn't look like it." He leaned his head back on the couch before he spoke again. "Do you want to open it, Emily?"

"Not until I calm down a little. I got so worked up about dinner…" I let my words trail off.

I hadn't been worked up about dinner, though, just frustrated. The real reason I'd been crying was because Trent had once again intruded on my life. I didn't understand why he hadn't just left me alone. He'd organized it so that I was no longer a member of the family, I was anathema to them all, and now he'd sent me a letter.

"I just want you to hold me for a couple of minutes. Then we can open the hateful thing. Because you know it's going to be hateful. It's from Trent. What else could it be?"

Dylan slid down beside me, and I pulled him close and let his warmth wrap around me, I found peace in his arms, and my mind quieted down. I didn't feel so stressed now, and life wasn't so overwhelming. All it took was being in Dylan's arms.

Finally, I knew I couldn't put it off any longer, and I took a deep breath.

"Okay, let's open it. Let's find out how he wants to wreck my life now."

Dylan continued to hold me, and I didn't fight him, but I knew that letter was there on that table, and that soon, I'd have to open it. For now, I'd live in the tranquility that only Dylan could give me. For a few minutes longer.

WHAT HAPPENS NEXT?

What more does he want?

Just as Emily thinks she is finally settling into her new life, she is about to discover there are more secrets and surprises waiting for her right around the corner...

Find Out More On
www.amazon.com/dp/B07R6RGYH7

ALSO BY SUMMER COOPER

Read Summer's sexiest and most popular romance books.

DARK DESIRES SERIES
Dark Desire
Dark Rules
Dark Secret
Dark Time
Dark Truth

An Amazon Top 100
A sexy romantic comedy
Somebody To Love

An Amazon Top 100
A 5-book billionaire romance box set

Filthy Rich
Summer's other box sets include:
Too Much To Love
Down Right Dirty

Mafia's Obsession
A hot mafia romance series
Mafia's Dirty Secret
Mafia's Fake Bride
Mafia's Final Play

Screaming Demons
An MC romance series full of suspense
Take Over
Rough Start
Rough Ride
Rough Choice
New Era
Rough Patch
Rough Return
Rough Road
New Territory
Rough Trip
Rough Night
Rough Love

Check out Summer's entire collection at
www.summercooper.com/books

Happy reading,
Summer Cooper
xoxo

ABOUT SUMMER COOPER

Thank you so much for reading. Without you, it wouldn't be possible for me to be a full-time author. I hope you enjoy reading my books as much as I do writing them.

Besides (obviously!) reading and writing, I also love cuddling my dogs, shouting at Alexa, being upside down (aka Yoga) and driving my family cray-cray!

Follow me on
Facebook | Instagram
Goodreads | Bookbub | Amazon

Get in touch at
hello@summercooper.com

www.summercooper.com